Fungus the Bogeyman

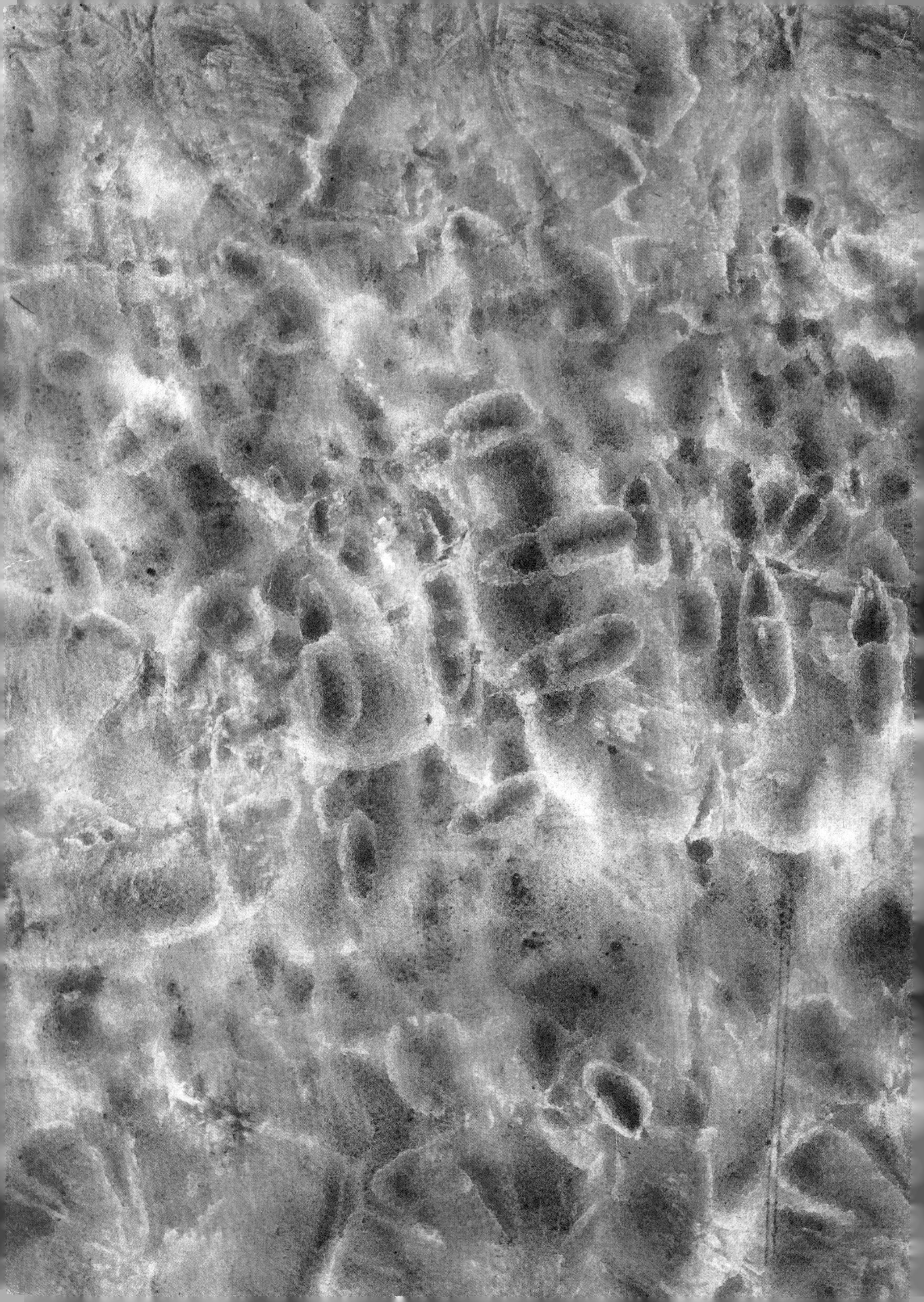

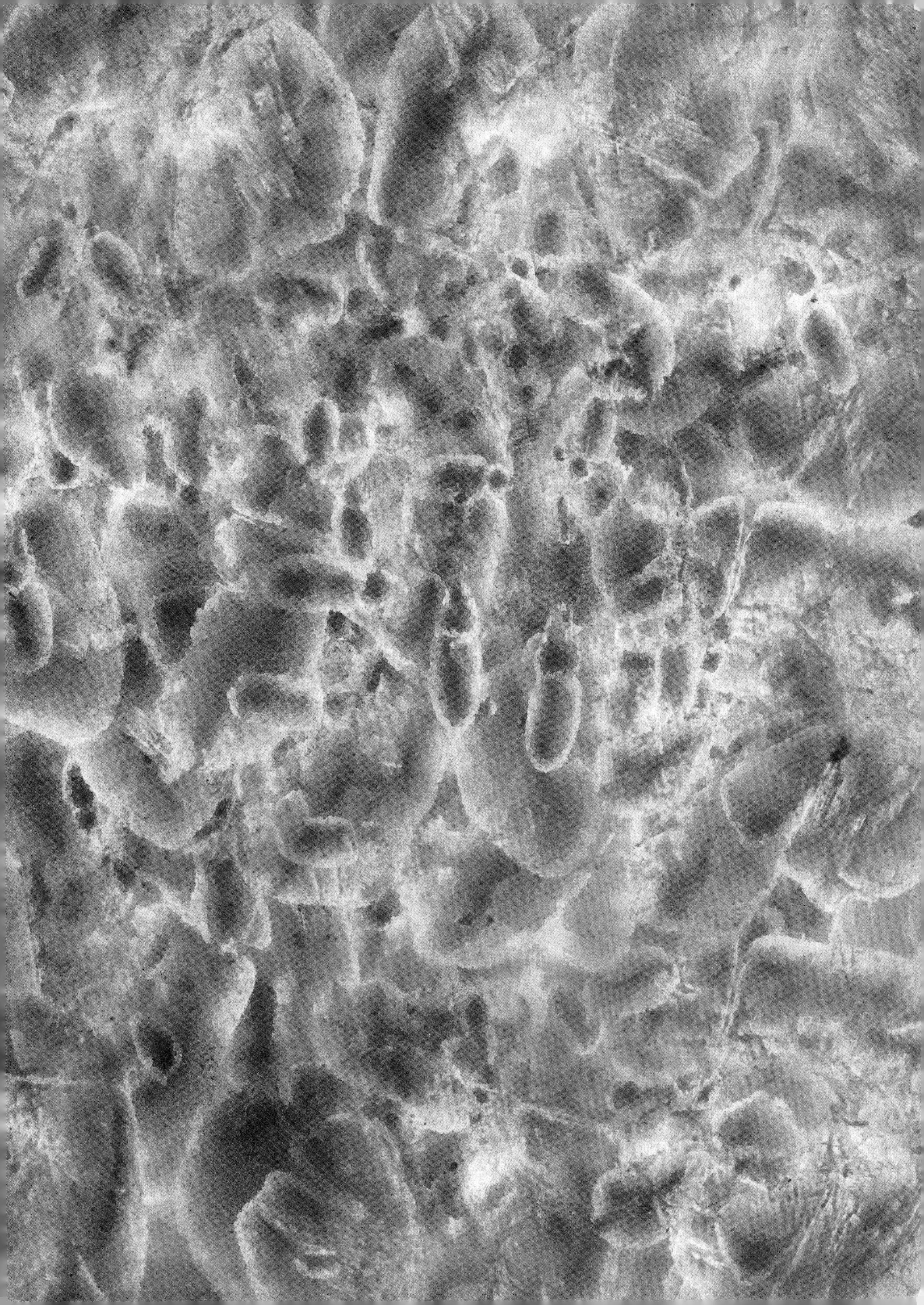

RAYMOND BRIGGS

Fungus the Bogeyman

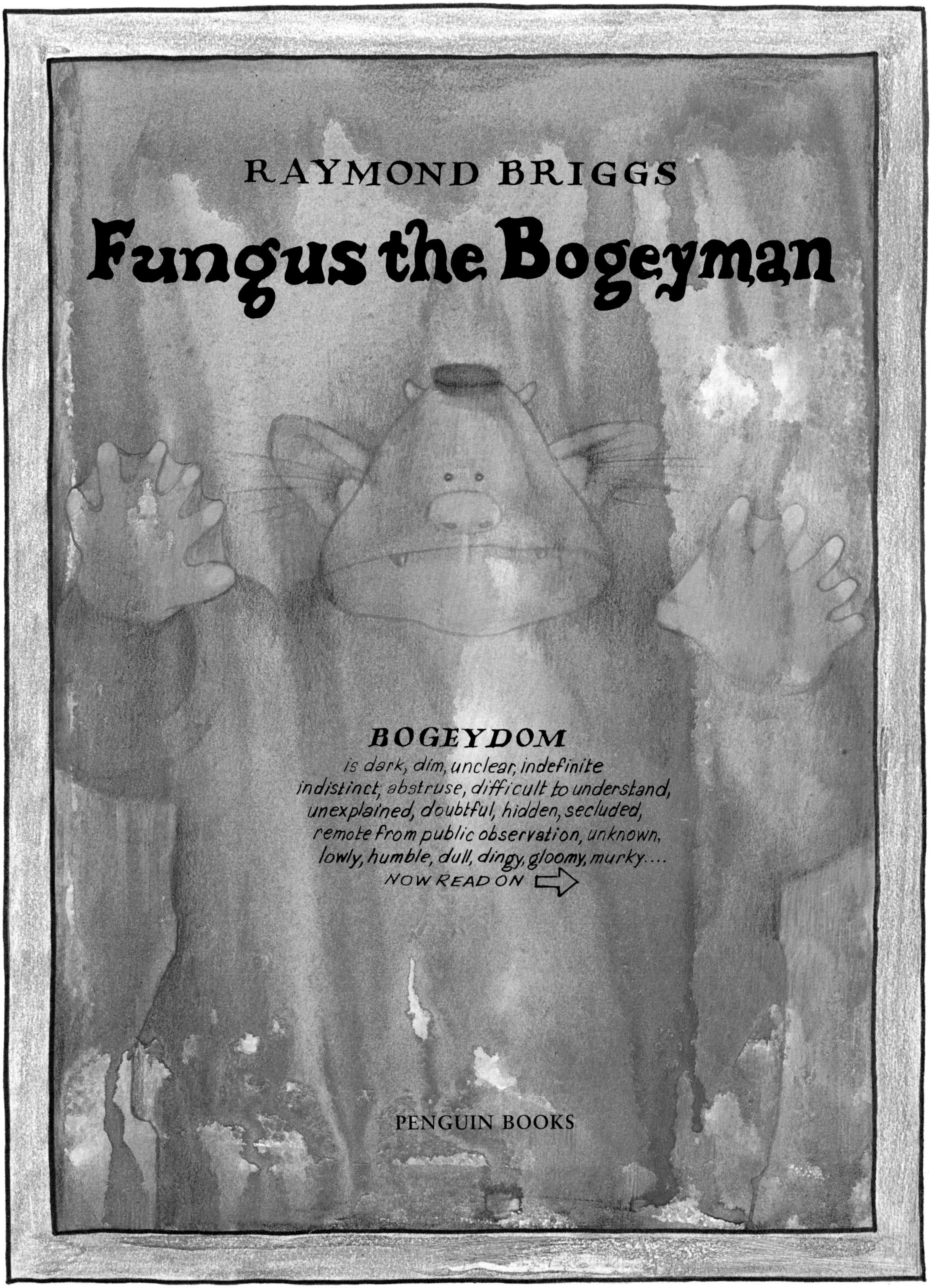

BOGEYDOM

is dark, dim, unclear, indefinite indistinct, abstruse, difficult to understand, unexplained, doubtful, hidden, secluded, remote from public observation, unknown, lowly, humble, dull, dingy, gloomy, murky....

NOW READ ON ⇨

PENGUIN BOOKS

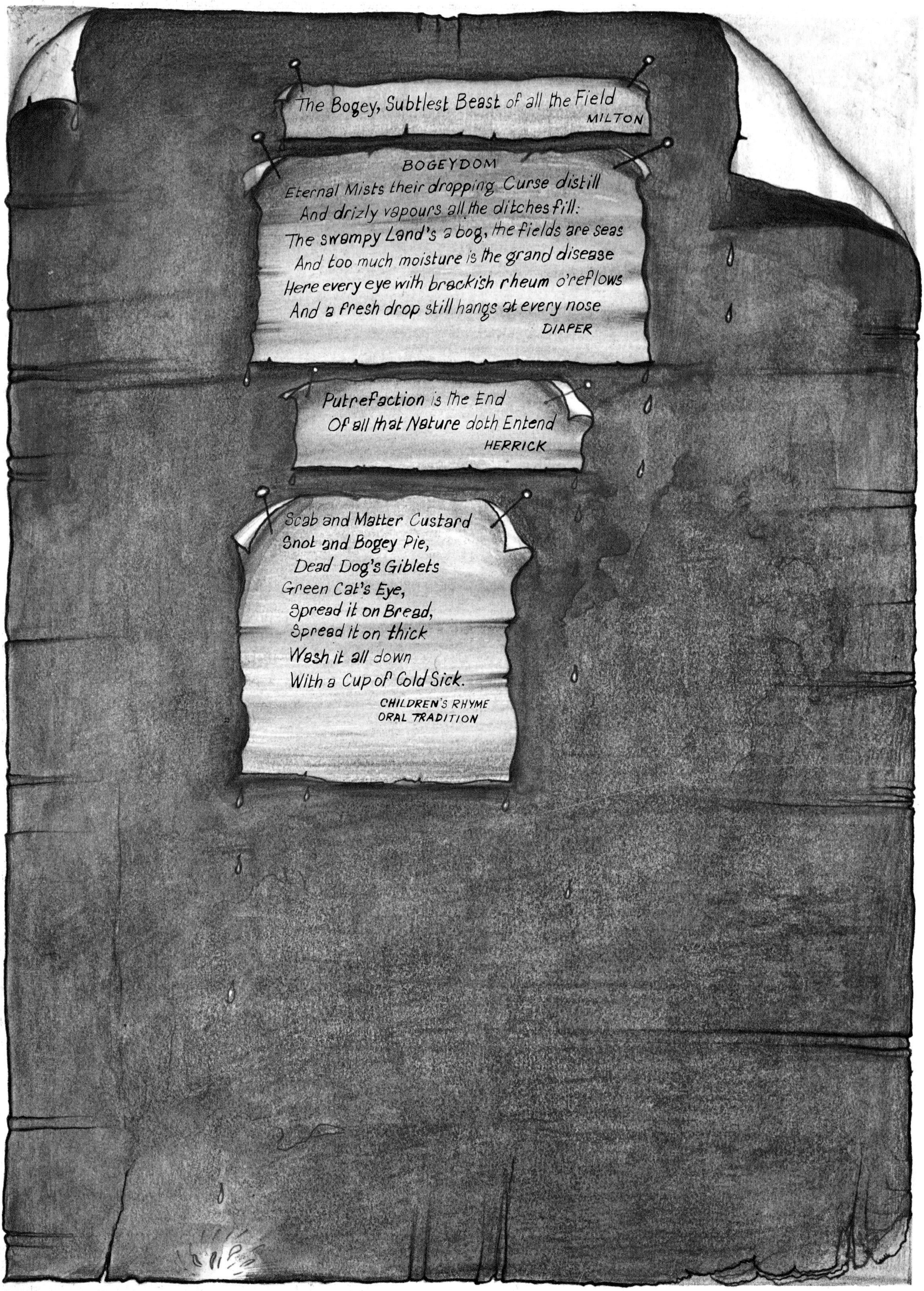

The Bogey, Subtlest Beast of all the Field
MILTON
BOGEYDOM
Eternal Mists their dropping Curse distill
And drizly vapours all the ditches fill:
The swampy Land's a bog, the fields are seas
And too much moisture is the grand disease
Here every eye with brackish rheum o'reflows
And a fresh drop still hangs at every nose
DIAPER
Putrefaction is the End
Of all that Nature doth Entend
HERRICK
Scab and Matter Custard
Snot and Bogey Pie,
Dead Dog's Giblets
Green Cat's Eye,
Spread it on Bread,
Spread it on thick
Wash it all down
With a Cup of Cold Sick.
CHILDREN'S RHYME
ORAL TRADITION

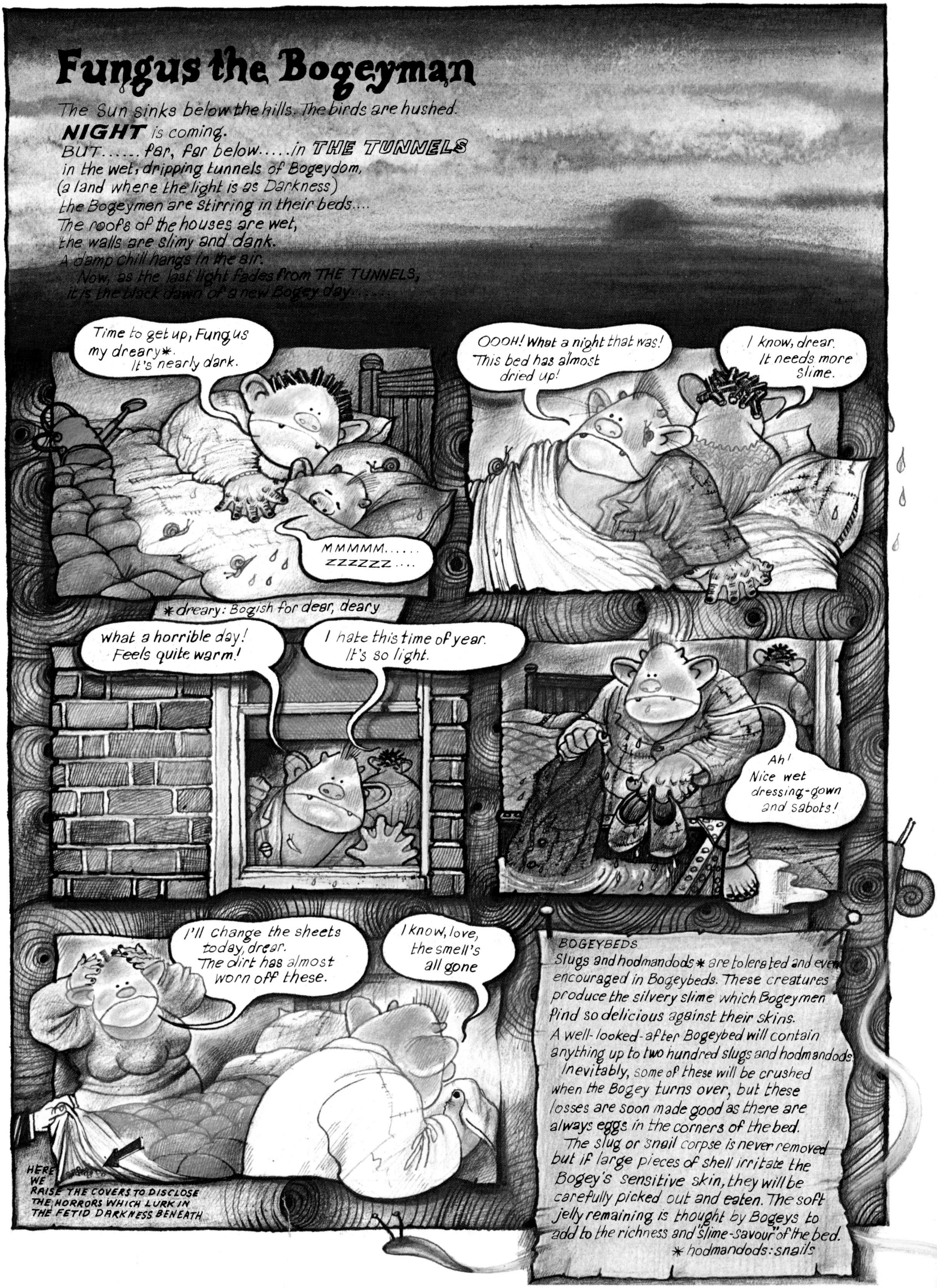
Fungus the Bogeyman
The Sun sinks below the hills. The birds are hushed.
NIGHT is coming.
BUT...... far, far below..... in THE TUNNELS
in the wet, dripping tunnels of Bogeydom,
(a land where the light is as Darkness)
the Bogeymen are stirring in their beds....
The roofs of the houses are wet,
the walls are slimy and dank.
A damp chill hangs in the air.
Now, as the last light fades from THE TUNNELS,
it's the black dawn of a new Bogey day......
Time to get up, Fungus my dreary*. It's nearly dark.
MMMMM...... ZZZZZZ....
OOOH! What a night that was! This bed has almost dried up!
I know, drear. It needs more slime.
* dreary: Bogish for dear, deary
What a horrible day! Feels quite warm!
I hate this time of year. It's so light.
Ah! Nice wet dressing-gown and sabots!
I'll change the sheets today, drear. The dirt has almost worn off these.
I know, love, the smell's all gone
HERE WE RAISE THE COVERS TO DISCLOSE THE HORRORS WHICH LURK IN THE FETID DARKNESS BENEATH
BOGEYBEDS
Slugs and hodmandods* are tolerated and even encouraged in Bogeybeds. These creatures produce the silvery slime which Bogeymen find so delicious against their skins.
A well-looked-after Bogeybed will contain anything up to two hundred slugs and hodmandods.
Inevitably, some of these will be crushed when the Bogey turns over, but these losses are soon made good as there are always eggs in the corners of the bed.
The slug or snail corpse is never removed but if large pieces of shell irritate the Bogey's sensitive skin, they will be carefully picked out and eaten. The soft jelly remaining is thought by Bogeys to add to the richness and "slime-savour" of the bed.
* hodmandods: snails

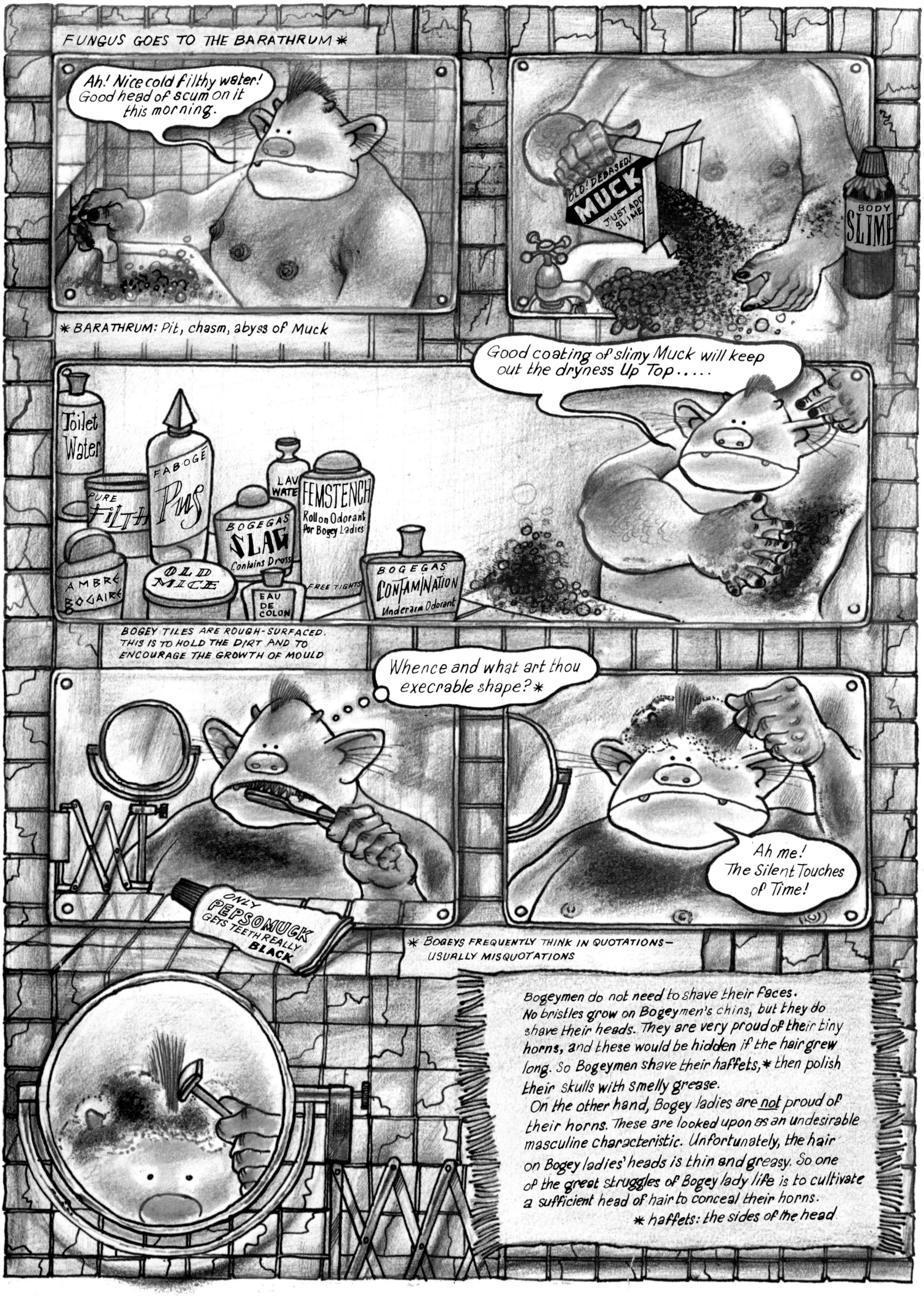
FUNGUS GOES TO THE BARATHRUM *
Ah! Nice cold filthy water! Good head of scum on it this morning.
OLD! DEBASED! MUCK JUST ADD SLIME
BODY SLIME
* BARATHRUM: Pit, chasm, abyss of Muck
Good coating of slimy Muck will keep out the dryness Up Top.....
Toilet Water
PURE FILTH
FABOGÉ Pus
BOGEGAS SLAG Contains Dross
FEMSTENCH Roll on Odorant For Bogey Ladies
FREE TIGHTS
AMBRE BOGAIRE
OLD MICE
EAU DE COLON
BOGEGAS CONTAMINATION Underarm Odorant
BOGEY TILES ARE ROUGH-SURFACED. THIS IS TO HOLD THE DIRT AND TO ENCOURAGE THE GROWTH OF MOULD
Whence and what art thou execrable shape? *
Ah me! The Silent Touches of Time!
ONLY PEPSOMUCK GETS TEETH REALLY BLACK
* BOGEYS FREQUENTLY THINK IN QUOTATIONS— USUALLY MISQUOTATIONS
Bogeymen do not need to shave their faces. No bristles grow on Bogeymen's chins, but they do shave their heads. They are very proud of their tiny horns, and these would be hidden if the hair grew long. So Bogeymen shave their haffets,* then polish their skulls with smelly grease.
On the other hand, Bogey ladies are not proud of their horns. These are looked upon as an undesirable masculine characteristic. Unfortunately, the hair on Bogey ladies' heads is thin and greasy. So one of the great struggles of Bogey lady life is to cultivate a sufficient head of hair to conceal their horns.
* haffets: the sides of the head

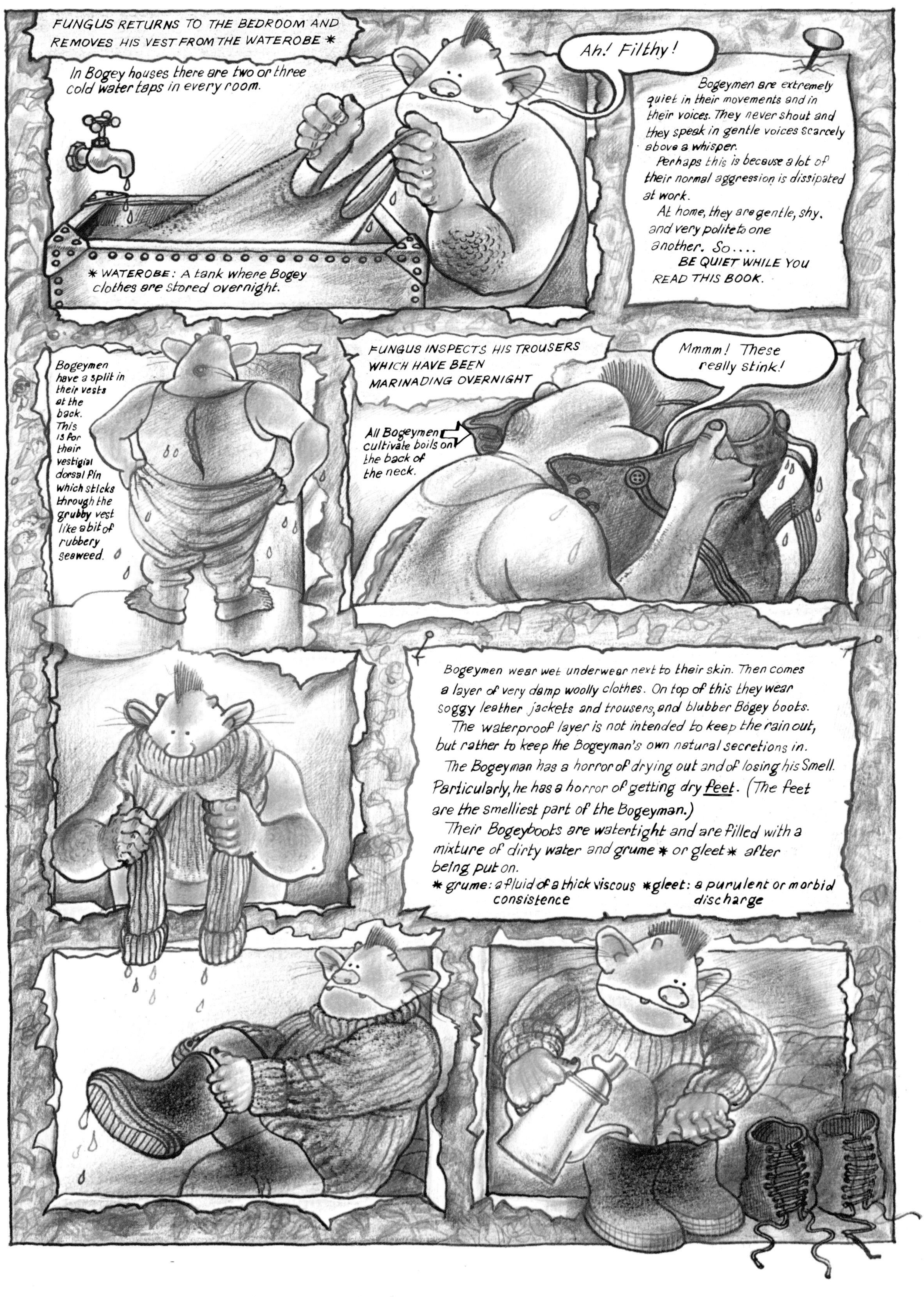

FUNGUS RETURNS TO THE BEDROOM AND REMOVES HIS VEST FROM THE WATEROBE *
In Bogey houses there are two or three cold water taps in every room.
* WATEROBE: A tank where Bogey clothes are stored overnight.
Ah! Filthy!
Bogeymen are extremely quiet in their movements and in their voices. They never shout and they speak in gentle voices scarcely above a whisper.
Perhaps this is because a lot of their normal aggression is dissipated at work.
At home, they are gentle, shy, and very polite to one another. So....
BE QUIET WHILE YOU READ THIS BOOK.
Bogeymen have a split in their vests at the back. This is for their vestigial dorsal fin which sticks through the grubby vest like a bit of rubbery seaweed.
FUNGUS INSPECTS HIS TROUSERS WHICH HAVE BEEN MARINADING OVERNIGHT
Mmmm! These really stink!
All Bogeymen cultivate boils on the back of the neck.
Bogeymen wear wet underwear next to their skin. Then comes a layer of very damp woolly clothes. On top of this they wear soggy leather jackets and trousers, and blubber Bogey boots.
The waterproof layer is not intended to keep the rain out, but rather to keep the Bogeyman's own natural secretions in.
The Bogeyman has a horror of drying out and of losing his Smell. Particularly, he has a horror of getting dry feet. (The feet are the smelliest part of the Bogeyman.)
Their Bogeyboots are watertight and are filled with a mixture of dirty water and grume * or gleet * after being put on.
* grume: a fluid of a thick viscous consistence
* gleet: a purulent or morbid discharge

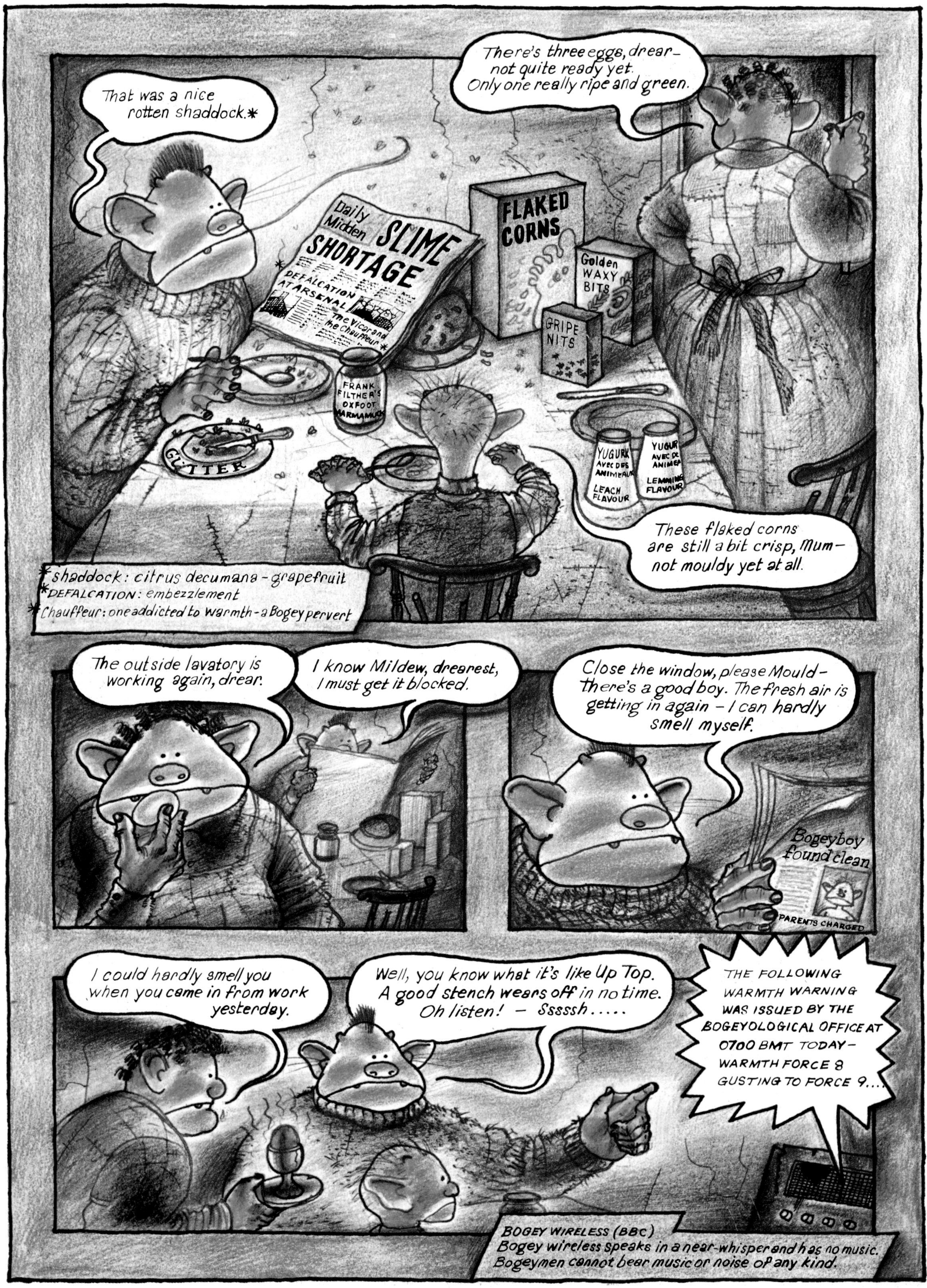
That was a nice rotten shaddock.*
There's three eggs, drear – not quite ready yet. Only one really ripe and green.
Daily Midden
SLIME SHORTAGE
DEFALCATION AT ARSENAL
The Vicar and the Chauffeur
FLAKED CORNS
Golden WAXY BITS
GRIPE NITS
FRANK FILTHER'S OXFOOT
GUTTER
YUGURK AVEC DES ANIMEAUX LEACH FLAVOUR
YUGURK AVEC DES ANIMEAUX LEMMING FLAVOUR
These flaked corns are still a bit crisp, Mum – not mouldy yet at all.
*shaddock: citrus decumana – grapefruit
*DEFALCATION: embezzlement
*Chauffeur: one addicted to warmth – a Bogey pervert
The outside lavatory is working again, drear.
I know Mildew, drearest, I must get it blocked.
Close the window, please Mould – there's a good boy. The fresh air is getting in again – I can hardly smell myself.
Bogeyboy found clean
PARENTS CHARGED
I could hardly smell you when you came in from work yesterday.
Well, you know what it's like Up Top. A good stench wears off in no time. Oh listen! – Ssssssh.....
THE FOLLOWING WARMTH WARNING WAS ISSUED BY THE BOGEYOLOGICAL OFFICE AT 0700 BMT TODAY – WARMTH FORCE 8 GUSTING TO FORCE 9....
BOGEY WIRELESS (BBC)
Bogey wireless speaks in a near-whisper and has no music. Bogeymen cannot bear music or noise of any kind.

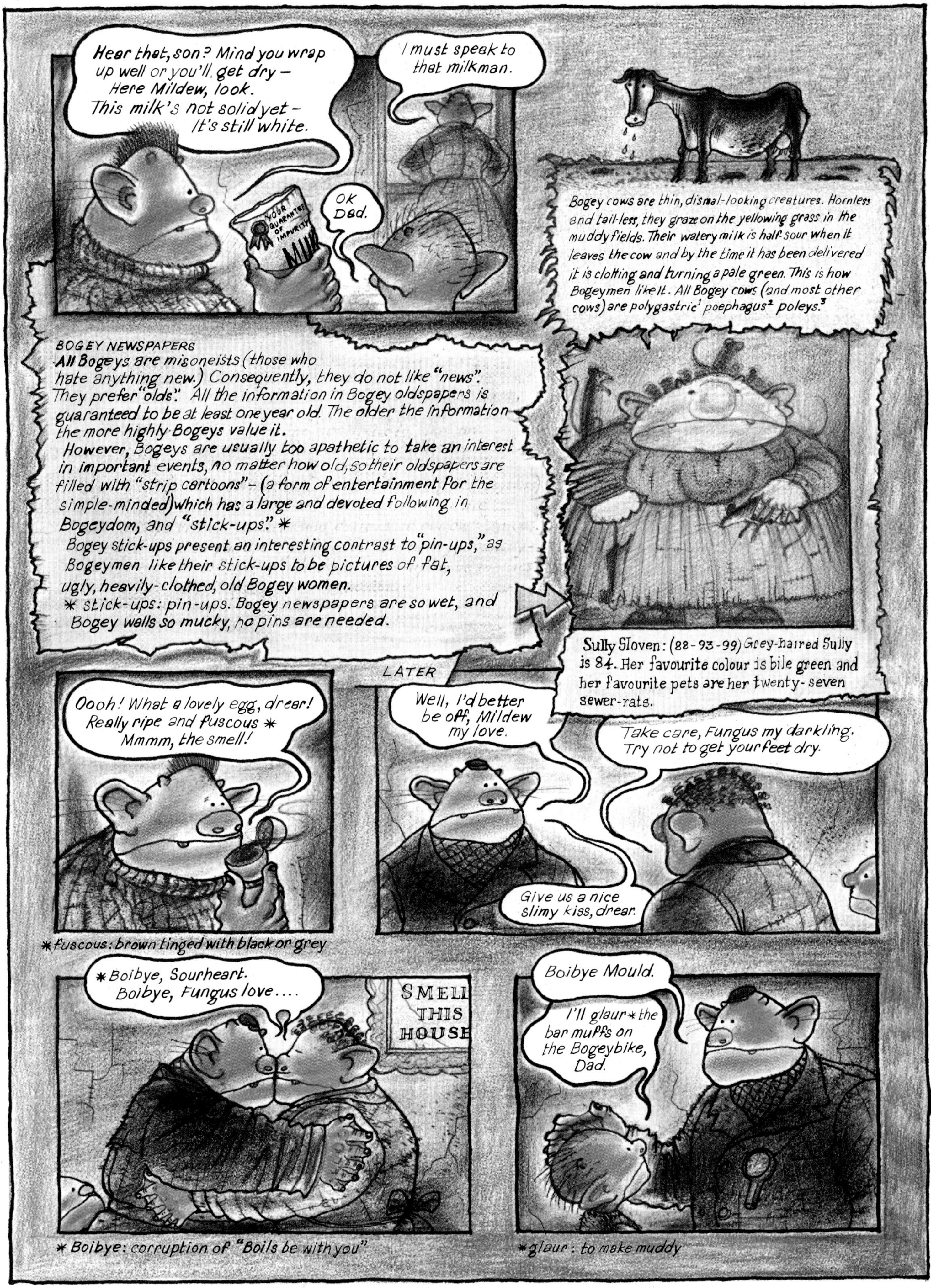
Hear that, son? Mind you wrap up well or you'll get dry – Here Mildew, look. This milk's not solid yet – It's still white.
YOUR GUARANTEE OF IMPURITY
MILK
I must speak to that milkman.
OK Dad.
Bogey cows are thin, dismal-looking creatures. Hornless and tail-less, they graze on the yellowing grass in the muddy fields. Their watery milk is half sour when it leaves the cow and by the time it has been delivered it is clotting and turning a pale green. This is how Bogeymen like it. All Bogey cows (and most other cows) are polygastric[1] poephagus[2] poleys.[3]
BOGEY NEWSPAPERS
All Bogeys are misoneists (those who hate anything new.) Consequently, they do not like "news". They prefer "olds". All the information in Bogey oldspapers is guaranteed to be at least one year old. The older the information the more highly Bogeys value it.
However, Bogeys are usually too apathetic to take an interest in important events, no matter how old, so their oldspapers are filled with "strip cartoons" – (a form of entertainment for the simple-minded) which has a large and devoted following in Bogeydom, and "stick-ups".*
Bogey stick-ups present an interesting contrast to "pin-ups," as Bogeymen like their stick-ups to be pictures of fat, ugly, heavily-clothed, old Bogey women.
* stick-ups: pin-ups. Bogey newspapers are so wet, and Bogey walls so mucky, no pins are needed.
Sully Sloven: (88-93-99) Grey-haired Sully is 84. Her favourite colour is bile green and her favourite pets are her twenty-seven sewer-rats.
Oooh! What a lovely egg, drear! Really ripe and fuscous * Mmmm, the smell!
*fuscous: brown tinged with black or grey
LATER
Well, I'd better be off, Mildew my love.
Take care, Fungus my darkling. Try not to get your feet dry.
Give us a nice slimy kiss, drear.
*Boibye, Sourheart. Boibye, Fungus love....
SMELL THIS HOUSE
*Boibye: corruption of "Boils be with you"
Boibye Mould.
I'll glaur* the bar muffs on the Bogeybike, Dad.
*glaur: to make muddy

1 polygastric: having many stomachs 2 poephagus: subsisting on grass 3 poleys: hornless (of cattle)

We must pause here to say a few words about Bogeybikes, as the bicycle is the principal means of transport in Bogeydom. Bogeys are far more interested in comfort than efficiency, so the most important part of a bicycle for them is the Saddle, or Bummle, as it is known.

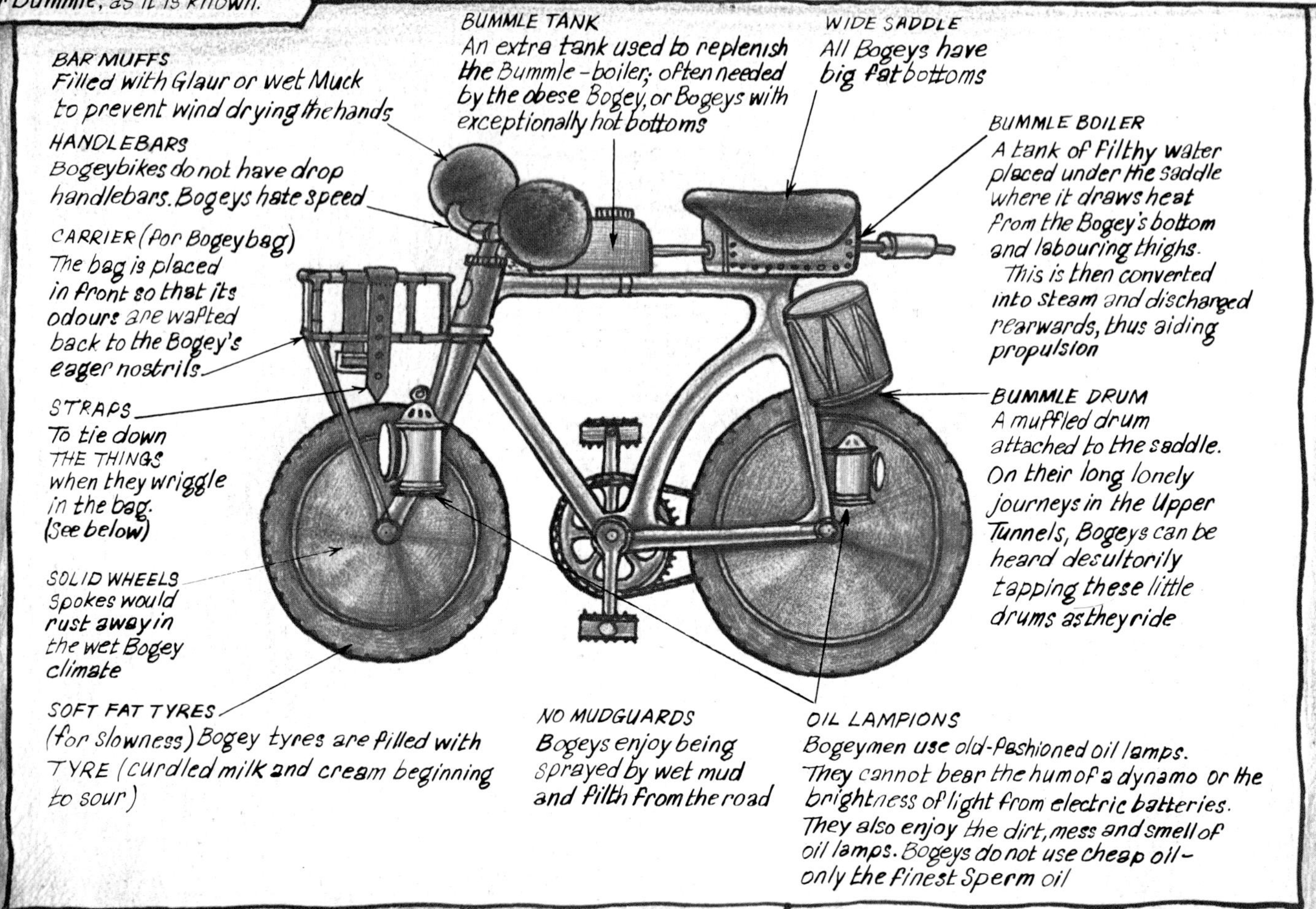

BUMMLE TANK
An extra tank used to replenish the Bummle-boiler; often needed by the obese Bogey, or Bogeys with exceptionally hot bottoms
WIDE SADDLE
All Bogeys have big fat bottoms
BAR MUFFS
Filled with Glaur or wet Muck to prevent wind drying the hands
HANDLEBARS
Bogeybikes do not have drop handlebars. Bogeys hate speed
CARRIER (for Bogeybag)
The bag is placed in front so that its odours are wafted back to the Bogey's eager nostrils
BUMMLE BOILER
A tank of filthy water placed under the saddle where it draws heat from the Bogey's bottom and labouring thighs. This is then converted into steam and discharged rearwards, thus aiding propulsion
STRAPS
To tie down THE THINGS when they wriggle in the bag. (See below)
BUMMLE DRUM
A muffled drum attached to the saddle. On their long lonely journeys in the Upper Tunnels, Bogeys can be heard desultorily tapping these little drums as they ride
SOLID WHEELS
Spokes would rust away in the wet Bogey climate
SOFT FAT TYRES
(for slowness) Bogey tyres are filled with TYRE (curdled milk and cream beginning to sour)
NO MUDGUARDS
Bogeys enjoy being sprayed by wet mud and filth from the road
OIL LAMPIONS
Bogeymen use old-fashioned oil lamps. They cannot bear the hum of a dynamo or the brightness of light from electric batteries. They also enjoy the dirt, mess and smell of oil lamps. Bogeys do not use cheap oil - only the finest Sperm oil

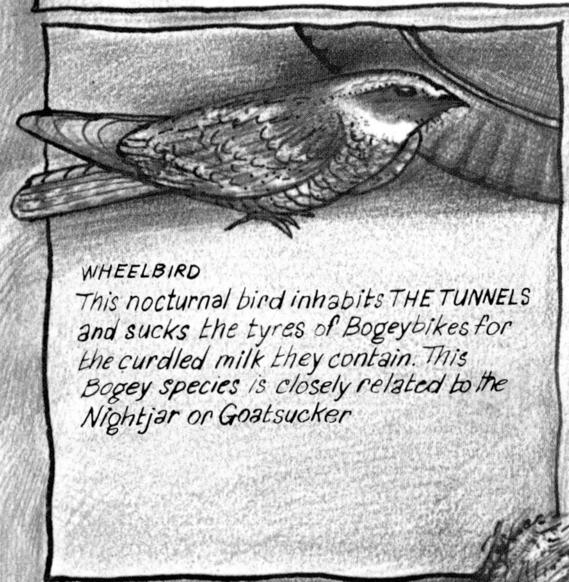

WHEELBIRD
This nocturnal bird inhabits THE TUNNELS and sucks the tyres of Bogeybikes for the curdled milk they contain. This Bogey species is closely related to the Nightjar or Goatsucker

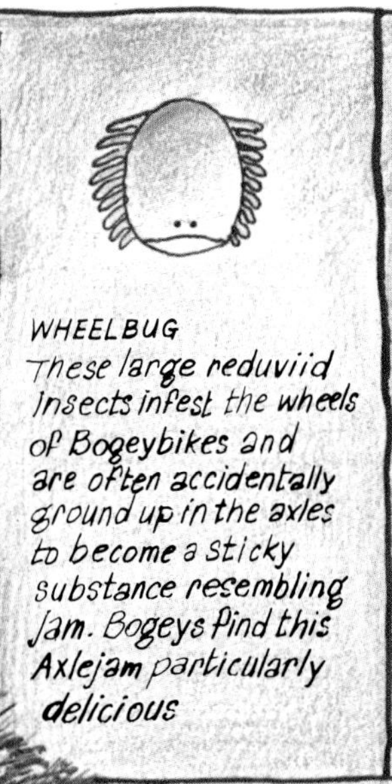

WHEELBUG
These large reduviid insects infest the wheels of Bogeybikes and are often accidentally ground up in the axles to become a sticky substance resembling jam. Bogeys find this Axlejam particularly delicious

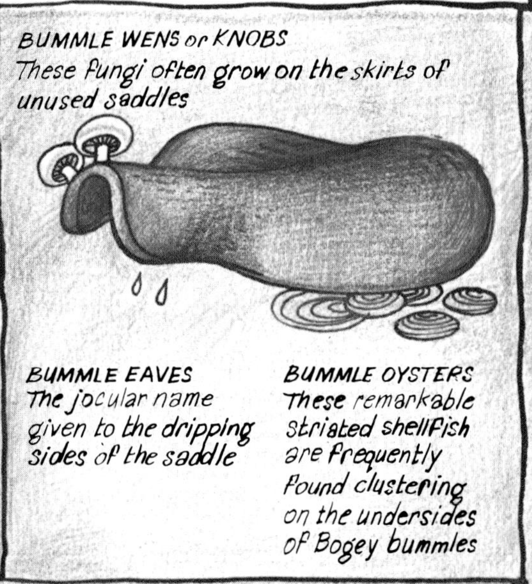

BUMMLE WENS or KNOBS
These fungi often grow on the skirts of unused saddles
BUMMLE EAVES
The jocular name given to the dripping sides of the saddle
BUMMLE OYSTERS
These remarkable striated shellfish are frequently found clustering on the undersides of Bogey bummles

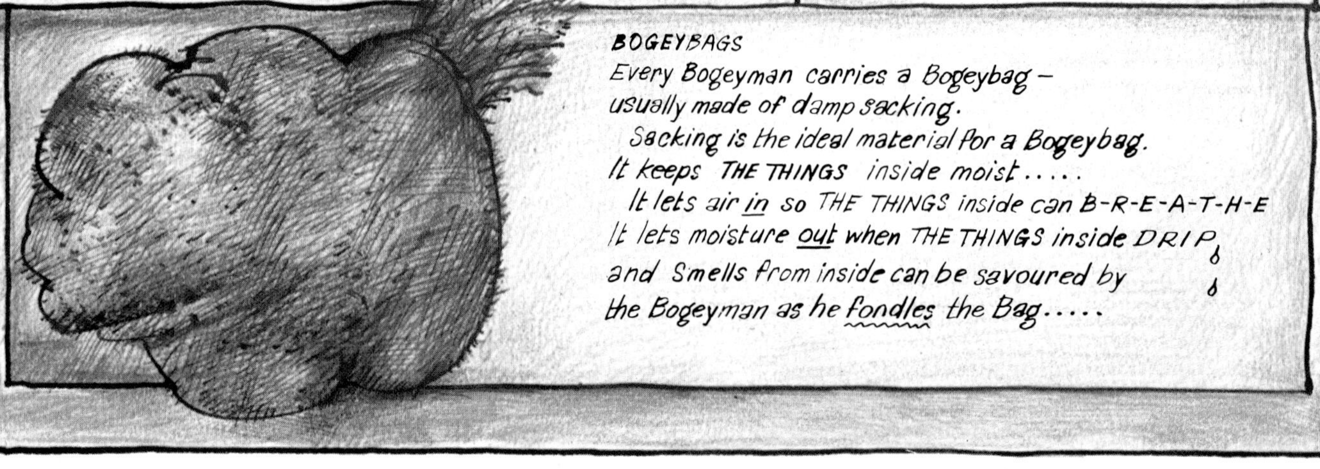

BOGEYBAGS
Every Bogeyman carries a Bogeybag - usually made of damp sacking.
Sacking is the ideal material for a Bogeybag.
It keeps THE THINGS inside moist.....
It lets air in so THE THINGS inside can B-R-E-A-T-H-E
It lets moisture out when THE THINGS inside DRIP
and Smells from inside can be savoured by the Bogeyman as he fondles the Bag.....

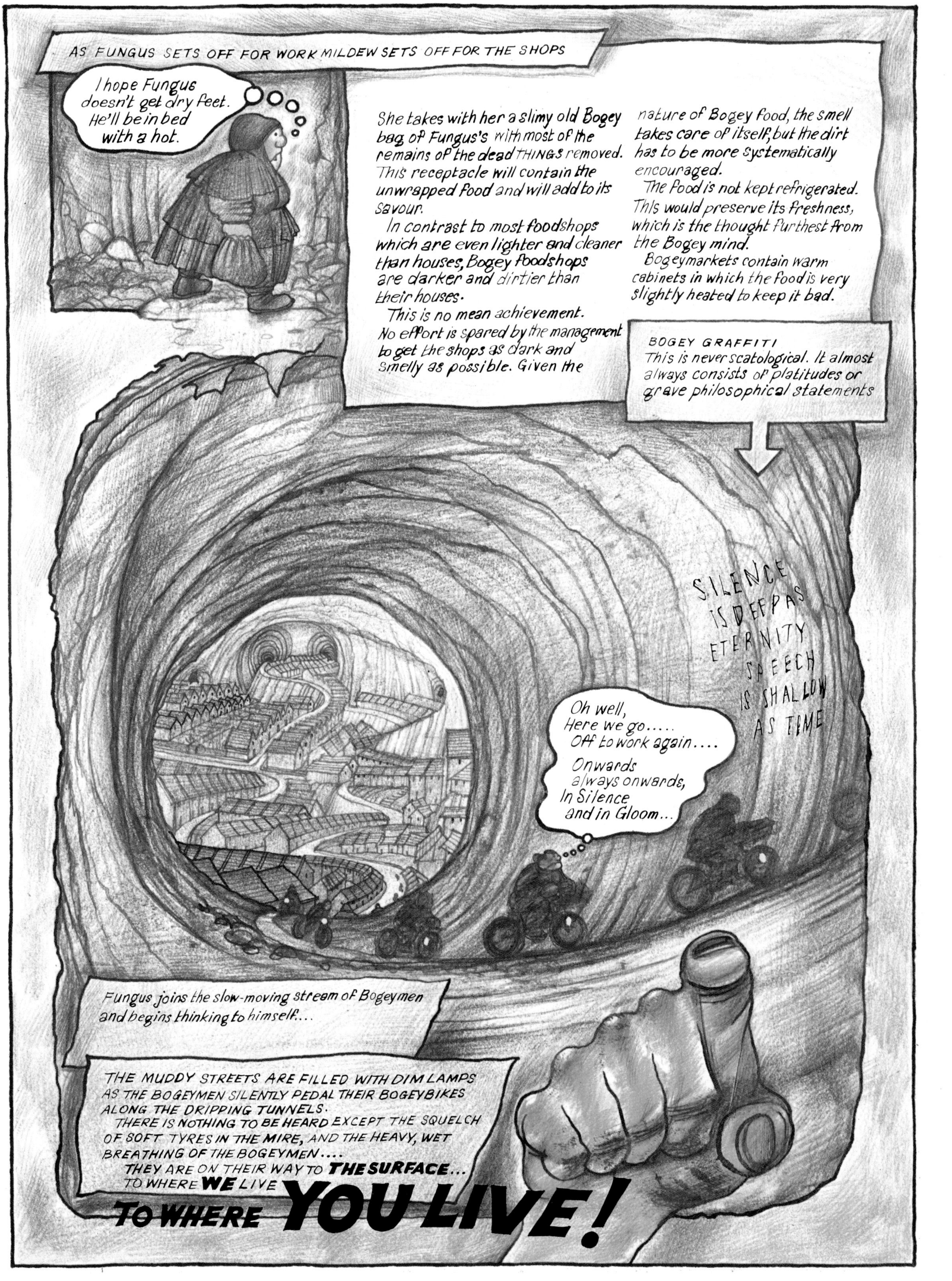
AS FUNGUS SETS OFF FOR WORK MILDEW SETS OFF FOR THE SHOPS
I hope Fungus doesn't get dry feet. He'll be in bed with a hot.
She takes with her a slimy old Bogey bag of Fungus's with most of the remains of the dead THINGS removed. This receptacle will contain the unwrapped food and will add to its savour.
In contrast to most foodshops which are even lighter and cleaner than houses, Bogey foodshops are darker and dirtier than their houses.
This is no mean achievement. No effort is spared by the management to get the shops as dark and smelly as possible. Given the nature of Bogey food, the smell takes care of itself, but the dirt has to be more systematically encouraged.
The food is not kept refrigerated. This would preserve its freshness, which is the thought furthest from the Bogey mind.
Bogeymarkets contain warm cabinets in which the food is very slightly heated to keep it bad.
BOGEY GRAFFITI
This is never scatological. It almost always consists of platitudes or grave philosophical statements
SILENCE IS DEEP AS ETERNITY SPEECH IS SHALLOW AS TIME
Oh well, Here we go..... Off to work again.... Onwards always onwards, In Silence and in Gloom...
Fungus joins the slow-moving stream of Bogeymen and begins thinking to himself...
THE MUDDY STREETS ARE FILLED WITH DIM LAMPS AS THE BOGEYMEN SILENTLY PEDAL THEIR BOGEYBIKES ALONG THE DRIPPING TUNNELS.
THERE IS NOTHING TO BE HEARD EXCEPT THE SQUELCH OF SOFT TYRES IN THE MIRE, AND THE HEAVY, WET BREATHING OF THE BOGEYMEN....
THEY ARE ON THEIR WAY TO THE SURFACE...
TO WHERE WE LIVE
TO WHERE YOU LIVE!

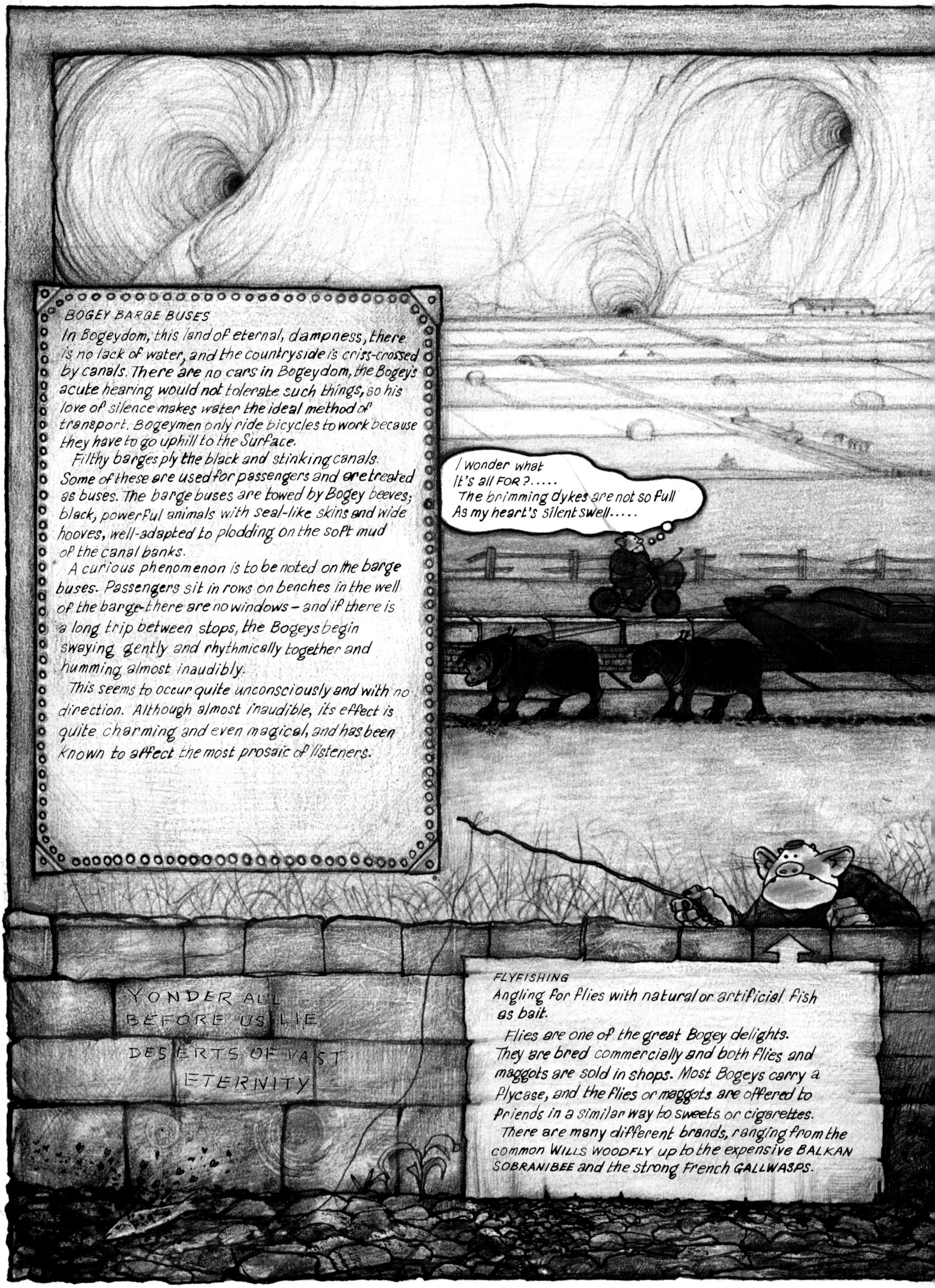
BOGEY BARGE BUSES
In Bogeydom, this land of eternal, dampness, there is no lack of water, and the countryside is criss-crossed by canals. There are no cars in Bogeydom, the Bogey's acute hearing would not tolerate such things, so his love of silence makes water the ideal method of transport. Bogeymen only ride bicycles to work because they have to go uphill to the Surface.
Filthy barges ply the black and stinking canals. Some of these are used for passengers and are treated as buses. The barge buses are towed by Bogey beeves; black, powerful animals with seal-like skins and wide hooves, well-adapted to plodding on the soft mud of the canal banks.
A curious phenomenon is to be noted on the barge buses. Passengers sit in rows on benches in the well of the barge-there are no windows – and if there is a long trip between stops, the Bogeys begin swaying gently and rhythmically together and humming almost inaudibly.
This seems to occur quite unconsciously and with no direction. Although almost inaudible, its effect is quite charming and even magical, and has been known to affect the most prosaic of listeners.
I wonder what it's all FOR?..... The brimming dykes are not so full As my heart's silent swell.....
YONDER ALL BEFORE US LIE DESERTS OF VAST ETERNITY
FLYFISHING
Angling for flies with natural or artificial fish as bait.
Flies are one of the great Bogey delights. They are bred commercially and both flies and maggots are sold in shops. Most Bogeys carry a flycase, and the flies or maggots are offered to friends in a similar way to sweets or cigarettes.
There are many different brands, ranging from the common WILLS WOODFLY up to the expensive BALKAN SOBRANIBEE and the strong French GALLWASPS.

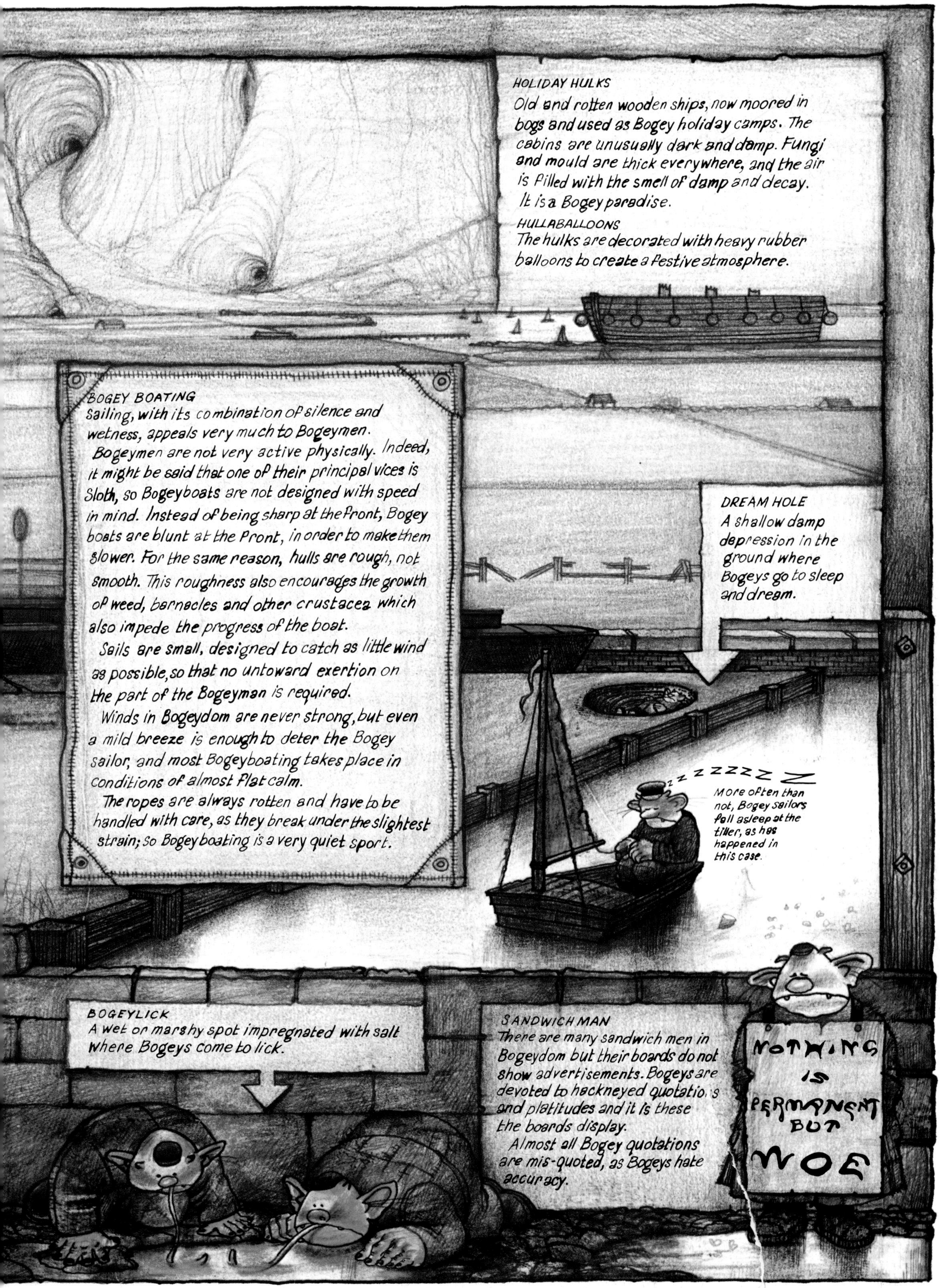
HOLIDAY HULKS
Old and rotten wooden ships, now moored in bogs and used as Bogey holiday camps. The cabins are unusually dark and damp. Fungi and mould are thick everywhere, and the air is filled with the smell of damp and decay. It is a Bogey paradise.
HULLABALLOONS
The hulks are decorated with heavy rubber balloons to create a festive atmosphere.
BOGEY BOATING
Sailing, with its combination of silence and wetness, appeals very much to Bogeymen.
Bogeymen are not very active physically. Indeed, it might be said that one of their principal vices is Sloth, so Bogeyboats are not designed with speed in mind. Instead of being sharp at the front, Bogey boats are blunt at the front, in order to make them slower. For the same reason, hulls are rough, not smooth. This roughness also encourages the growth of weed, barnacles and other crustacea which also impede the progress of the boat.
Sails are small, designed to catch as little wind as possible, so that no untoward exertion on the part of the Bogeyman is required.
Winds in Bogeydom are never strong, but even a mild breeze is enough to deter the Bogey sailor, and most Bogeyboating takes place in conditions of almost flat calm.
The ropes are always rotten and have to be handled with care, as they break under the slightest strain; so Bogey boating is a very quiet sport.
DREAM HOLE
A shallow damp depression in the ground where Bogeys go to sleep and dream.
zzzzzzzZZ
More often than not, Bogey sailors fall asleep at the tiller, as has happened in this case.
BOGEYLICK
A wet or marshy spot impregnated with salt where Bogeys come to lick.
SANDWICH MAN
There are many sandwich men in Bogeydom but their boards do not show advertisements. Bogeys are devoted to hackneyed quotations and platitudes and it is these the boards display.
Almost all Bogey quotations are mis-quoted, as Bogeys hate accuracy.
NOTHING IS PERMANENT BUT WOE

FUNGUS CYCLES ON PAST AN ODEUM

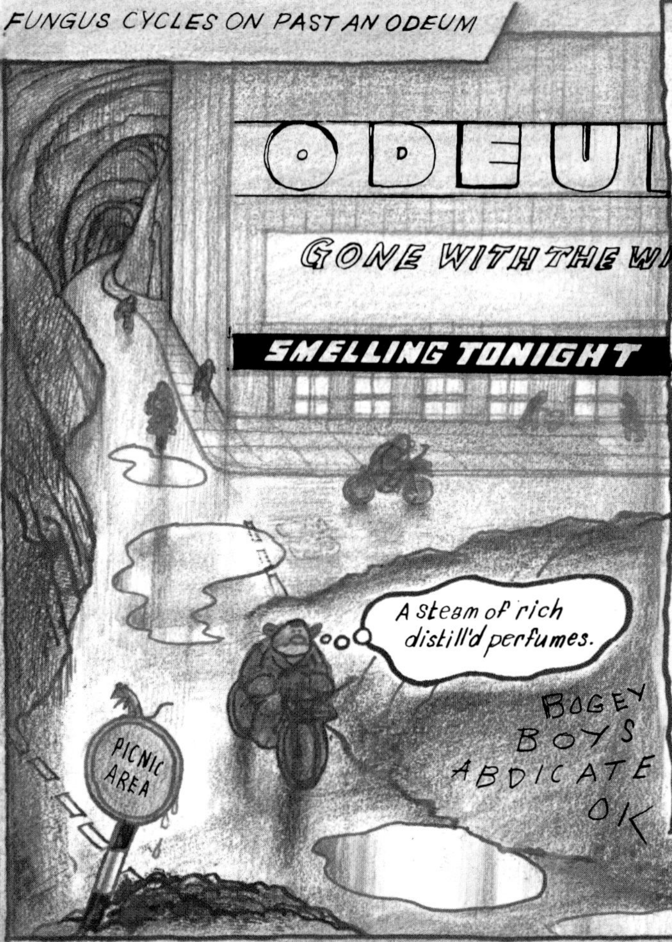
ODEU
GONE WITH THE W
SMELLING TONIGHT
A steam of rich distill'd perfumes.
PICNIC AREA
BOGEY BOYS ABDICATE OK

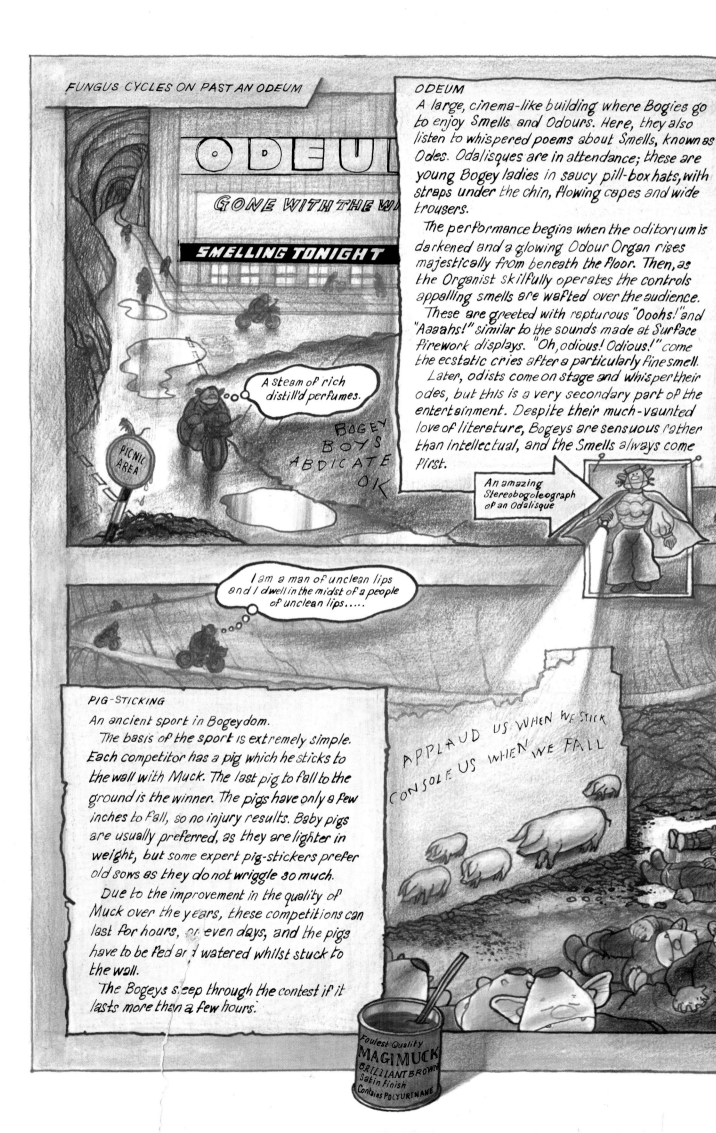

ODEUM

A large, cinema-like building where Bogies go to enjoy Smells and Odours. Here, they also listen to whispered poems about Smells, known as Odes. Odalisques are in attendance; these are young Bogey ladies in saucy pill-box hats, with straps under the chin, flowing capes and wide trousers.

The performance begins when the oditorium is darkened and a glowing Odour Organ rises majestically from beneath the floor. Then, as the Organist skilfully operates the controls appalling smells are wafted over the audience.

These are greeted with rapturous "Ooohs!" and "Aaaahs!" similar to the sounds made at Surface firework displays. "Oh, odious! Odious!" come the ecstatic cries after a particularly fine smell.

Later, odists come on stage and whisper their odes, but this is a very secondary part of the entertainment. Despite their much-vaunted love of literature, Bogeys are sensuous rather than intellectual, and the Smells always come first.

An amazing Stereobogoleograph of an Odalisque

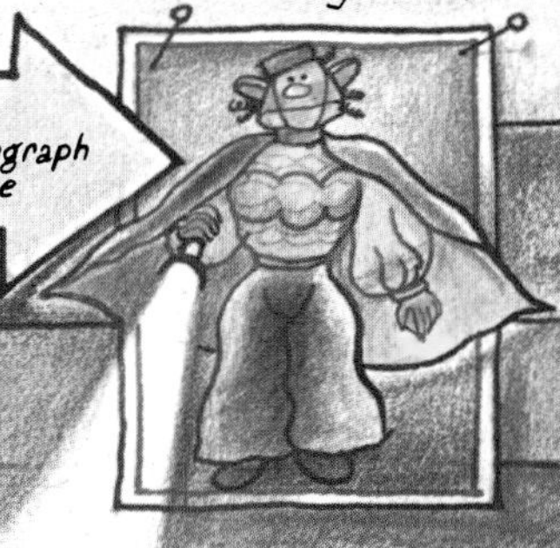

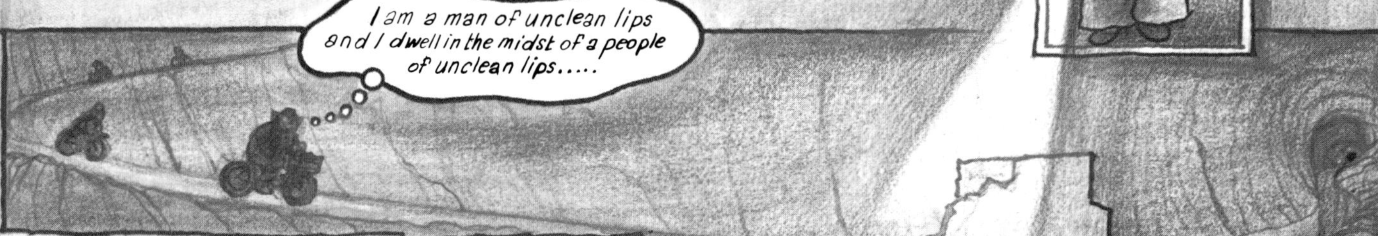
I am a man of unclean lips and I dwell in the midst of a people of unclean lips.....

PIG-STICKING

An ancient sport in Bogeydom.

The basis of the sport is extremely simple. Each competitor has a pig which he sticks to the wall with Muck. The last pig to fall to the ground is the winner. The pigs have only a few inches to fall, so no injury results. Baby pigs are usually preferred, as they are lighter in weight, but some expert pig-stickers prefer old sows as they do not wriggle so much.

Due to the improvement in the quality of Muck over the years, these competitions can last for hours, or even days, and the pigs have to be fed and watered whilst stuck to the wall.

The Bogeys sleep through the contest if it lasts more than a few hours.

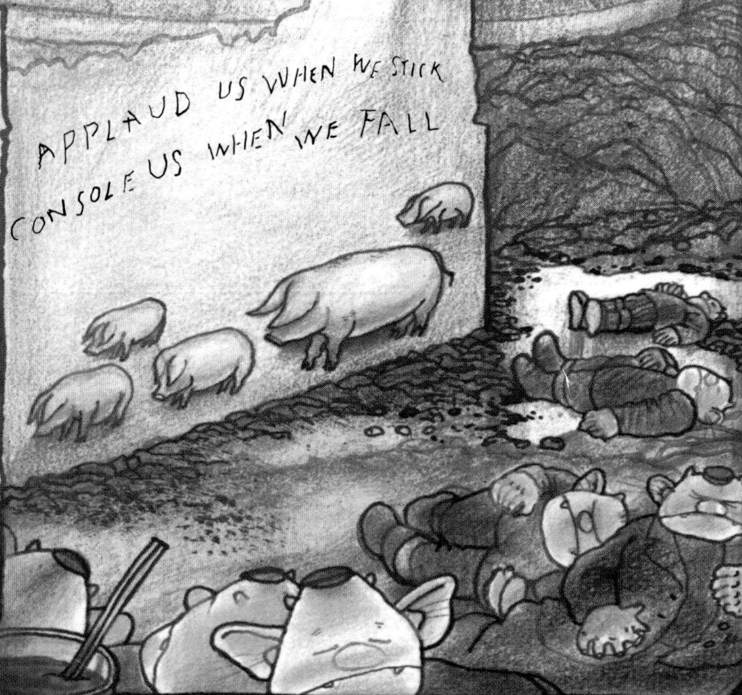
APPLAUD US WHEN WE STICK
CONSOLE US WHEN WE FALL
Foulest Quality
MAGIMUCK
BRILLIANT BROWN
Satin Finish
Contains POLYURINANE

YE OLDE BOGEY BATTERYES

These ancient structures are found near the borders of Bogeydom, and were made for defence against Napoleybogey.

The walls of the batteries were built of soggy Muck to make them difficult for the enemy to climb. The Quaker Guns * at the top were calculated to inspire fear in the hearts of the enemy when viewed from a distance. (All Bogey guns are made of wood. They make no noise, have no ammunition, and do not fire. Long ago, Bogeys realised that metal guns did far more harm than good, so wooden ones were introduced. These have been found to be much more satisfactory, as they are silent and harmless.)

However, the wooden guns were so rotten, they fell to pieces when ever they were moved. The dummy wooden cannon balls were used by the gunners for playing bowels (Bogey bowls) though they were of little use even for this purpose, because they were <u>Bogey</u> balls and therefore not round and consequently rolled about in a promiscuous fashion.

As the Bogeys had no idea from which direction Napoleybogey would come, the Quaker Guns were, of course, quaquaversal.

* QUAKER GUN: a wooden gun mounted to deceive the enemy.

Long is the way And hard, that out of here leads up to light.

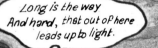

RUIN UPON RUIN ROUT ON ROUT

KEEP ON THE GRASS

POSTERS

Bogey posters do not advertise coming events; they advertise past events. By the time a Bogey sees the poster, the event which it announces has long since passed. Consequently, he does not need to write down times and dates, book tickets or travel, and can thus proceed with his normal indolent life in peace.

TIDDLYWINKS

Bogeymen are devoted to the game of Tiddlywinks, probably because it is silent and requires no exertion. As with most Bogey games, the object is to achieve a draw. This is not difficult, as Bogey tiddlywinks are made, not of bone, but of dried Muck. As a result, they usually snap in two when pressed one against the other and in damp weather they become soggy and useless.

The pot into which the tiddlywinks are aimed is filled with dirty water and if, by any chance a tiddlywink should fall into the pot, it instantly dissolves.

This seat of desolation void of light.

LAST WEEK!

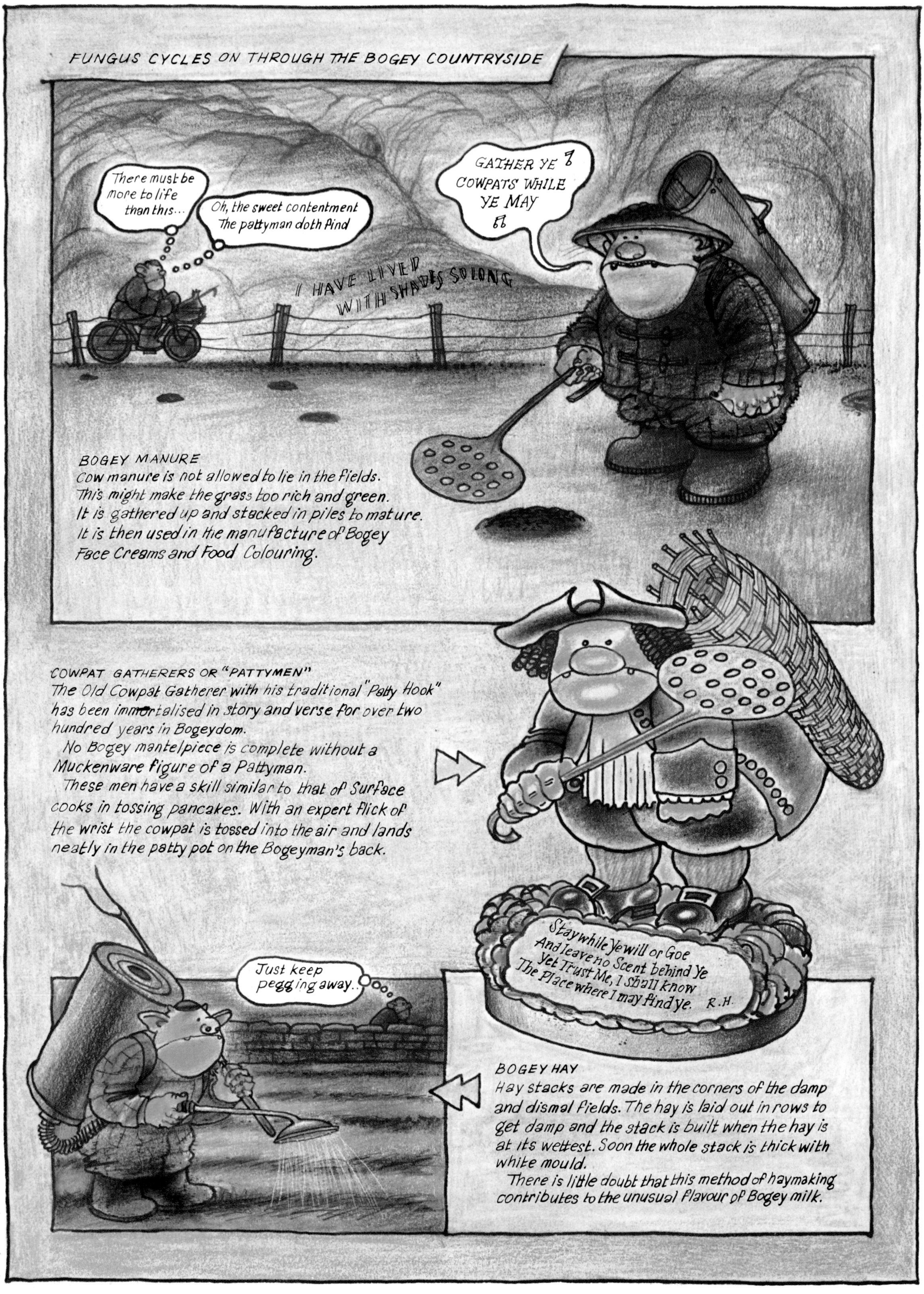
FUNGUS CYCLES ON THROUGH THE BOGEY COUNTRYSIDE
There must be more to life than this...
Oh, the sweet contentment The pattyman doth find
GATHER YE COWPATS WHILE YE MAY
I HAVE LIVED WITH SHADES SO LONG
BOGEY MANURE
Cow manure is not allowed to lie in the fields. This might make the grass too rich and green. It is gathered up and stacked in piles to mature. It is then used in the manufacture of Bogey Face Creams and Food Colouring.
COWPAT GATHERERS OR "PATTYMEN"
The Old Cowpat Gatherer with his traditional "Patty Hook" has been immortalised in story and verse for over two hundred years in Bogeydom.
No Bogey mantelpiece is complete without a Muckenware figure of a Pattyman.
These men have a skill similar to that of Surface cooks in tossing pancakes. With an expert flick of the wrist the cowpat is tossed into the air and lands neatly in the patty pot on the Bogeyman's back.
Stay while Ye will or Goe
And leave no Scent behind Ye
Yet Trust Me, I shall know
The Place where I may find ye.
R.H.
Just keep pegging away...
BOGEY HAY
Hay stacks are made in the corners of the damp and dismal fields. The hay is laid out in rows to get damp and the stack is built when the hay is at its wettest. Soon the whole stack is thick with white mould.
There is little doubt that this method of haymaking contributes to the unusual flavour of Bogey milk.

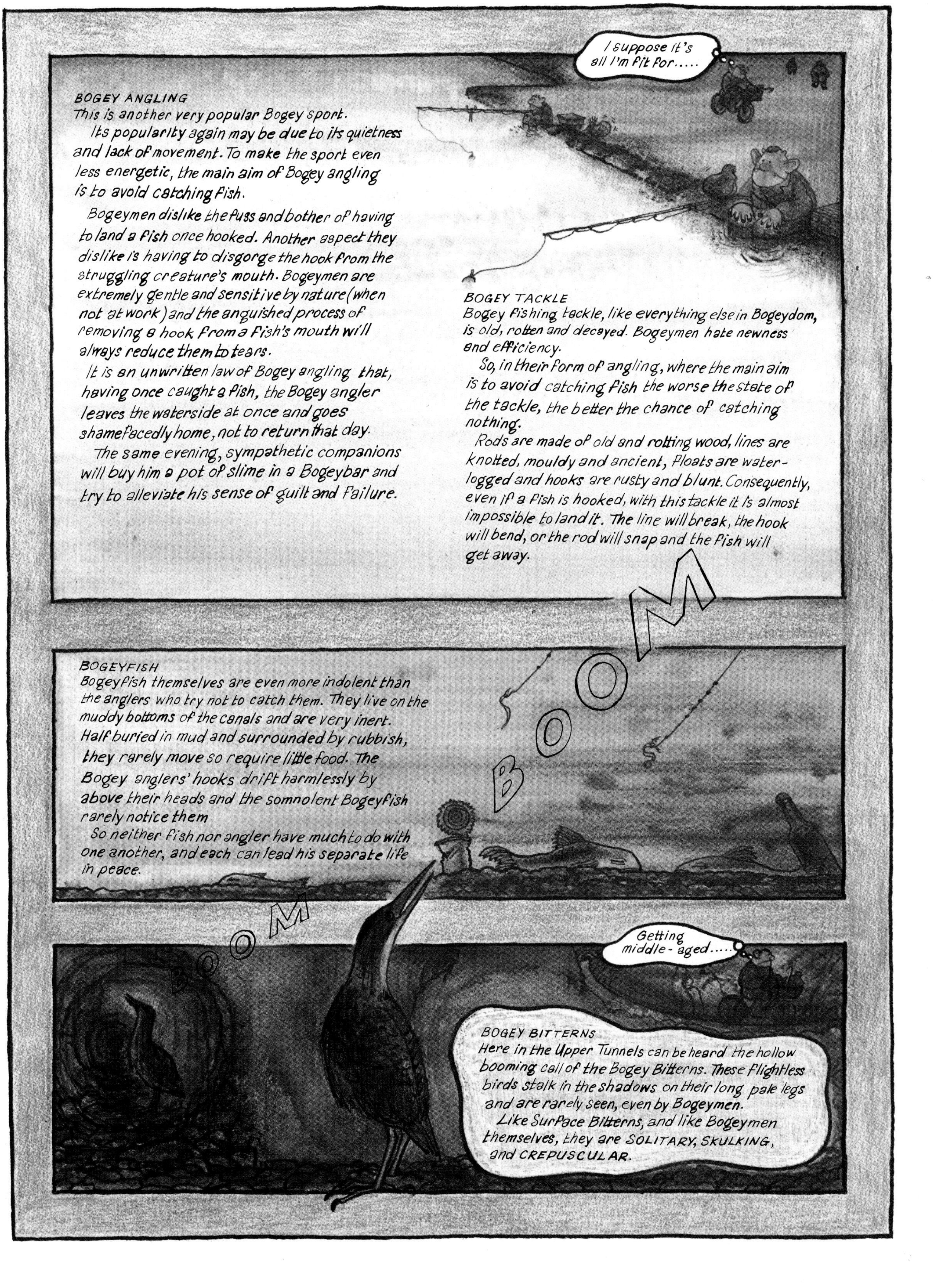
I suppose it's all I'm fit for.....
BOGEY ANGLING
This is another very popular Bogey sport.
Its popularity again may be due to its quietness and lack of movement. To make the sport even less energetic, the main aim of Bogey angling is to avoid catching fish.
Bogeymen dislike the fuss and bother of having to land a fish once hooked. Another aspect they dislike is having to disgorge the hook from the struggling creature's mouth. Bogeymen are extremely gentle and sensitive by nature (when not at work) and the anguished process of removing a hook from a fish's mouth will always reduce them to tears.
It is an unwritten law of Bogey angling that, having once caught a fish, the Bogey angler leaves the waterside at once and goes shamefacedly home, not to return that day.
The same evening, sympathetic companions will buy him a pot of slime in a Bogeybar and try to alleviate his sense of guilt and failure.
BOGEY TACKLE
Bogey fishing tackle, like everything else in Bogeydom, is old, rotten and decayed. Bogeymen hate newness and efficiency.
So, in their form of angling, where the main aim is to avoid catching fish the worse the state of the tackle, the better the chance of catching nothing.
Rods are made of old and rotting wood, lines are knotted, mouldy and ancient, floats are water-logged and hooks are rusty and blunt. Consequently, even if a fish is hooked, with this tackle it is almost impossible to land it. The line will break, the hook will bend, or the rod will snap and the fish will get away.
BOGEYFISH
Bogeyfish themselves are even more indolent than the anglers who try not to catch them. They live on the muddy bottoms of the canals and are very inert. Half buried in mud and surrounded by rubbish, they rarely move so require little food. The Bogey anglers' hooks drift harmlessly by above their heads and the somnolent Bogeyfish rarely notice them
So neither fish nor angler have much to do with one another, and each can lead his separate life in peace.
BOOM
BOOM
Getting middle-aged.....
BOGEY BITTERNS
Here in the Upper Tunnels can be heard the hollow booming call of the Bogey Bitterns. These flightless birds stalk in the shadows on their long pale legs and are rarely seen, even by Bogeymen.
Like Surface Bitterns, and like Bogeymen themselves, they are SOLITARY, SKULKING, and CREPUSCULAR.

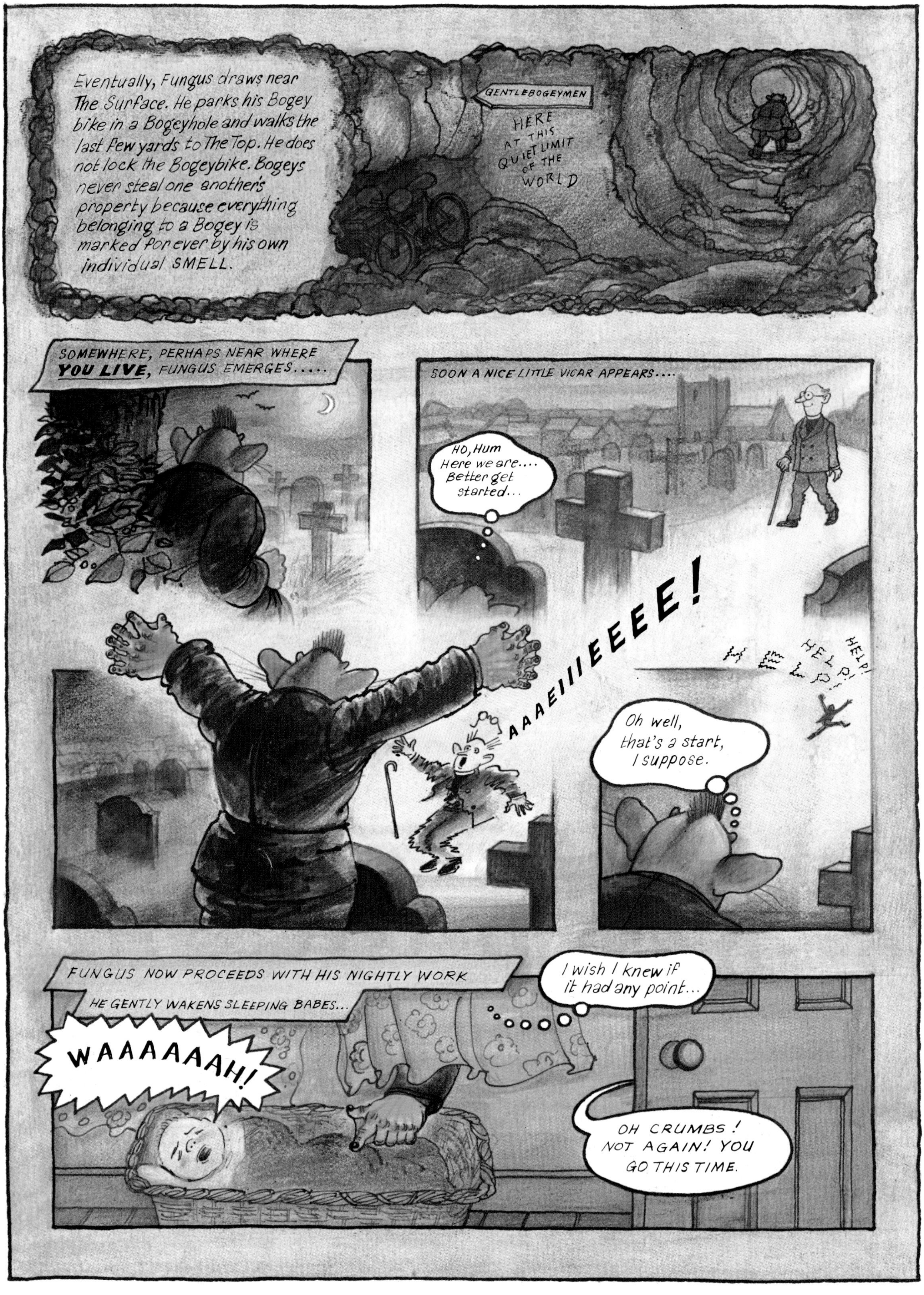

Eventually, Fungus draws near The Surface. He parks his Bogey bike in a Bogeyhole and walks the last few yards to The Top. He does not lock the Bogeybike. Bogeys never steal one another's property because everything belonging to a Bogey is marked for ever by his own individual SMELL.
GENTLEBOGEYMEN
HERE AT THIS QUIET LIMIT OF THE WORLD
SOMEWHERE, PERHAPS NEAR WHERE YOU LIVE, FUNGUS EMERGES.....
SOON A NICE LITTLE VICAR APPEARS....
HO, Hum Here we are.... Better get started...
AAAEIIIEEEE!
HELP! HELP!
Oh well, that's a start, I suppose.
FUNGUS NOW PROCEEDS WITH HIS NIGHTLY WORK
HE GENTLY WAKENS SLEEPING BABES...
I wish I knew if it had any point...
WAAAAAAH!
OH CRUMBS! NOT AGAIN! YOU GO THIS TIME.

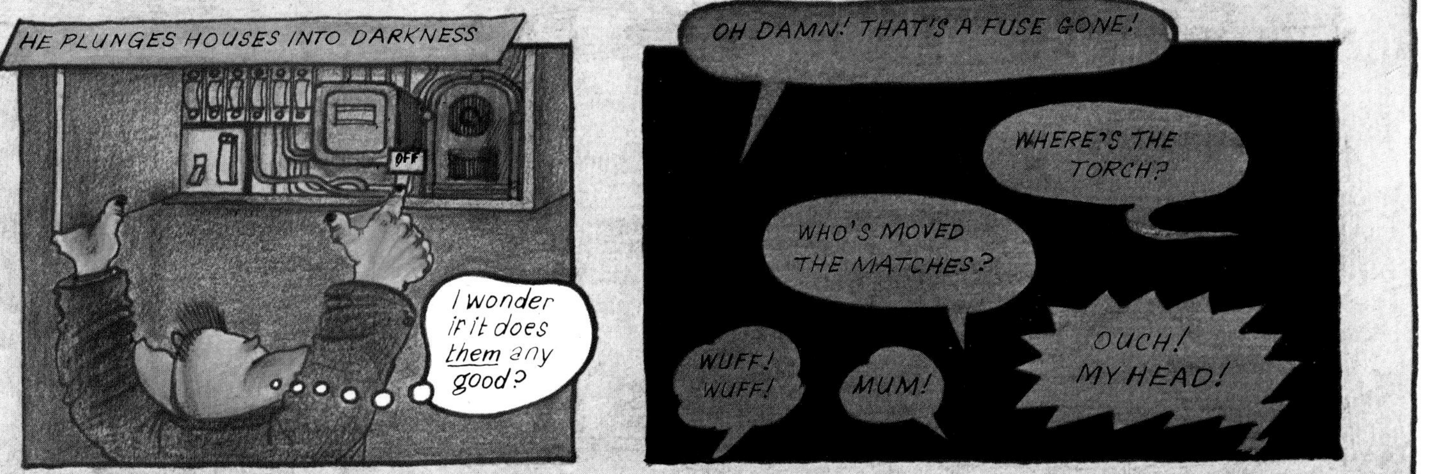
HE PLUNGES HOUSES INTO DARKNESS
OFF
I wonder if it does them any good?
OH DAMN! THAT'S A FUSE GONE!
WHERE'S THE TORCH?
WHO'S MOVED THE MATCHES?
WUFF! WUFF!
MUM!
OUCH! MY HEAD!

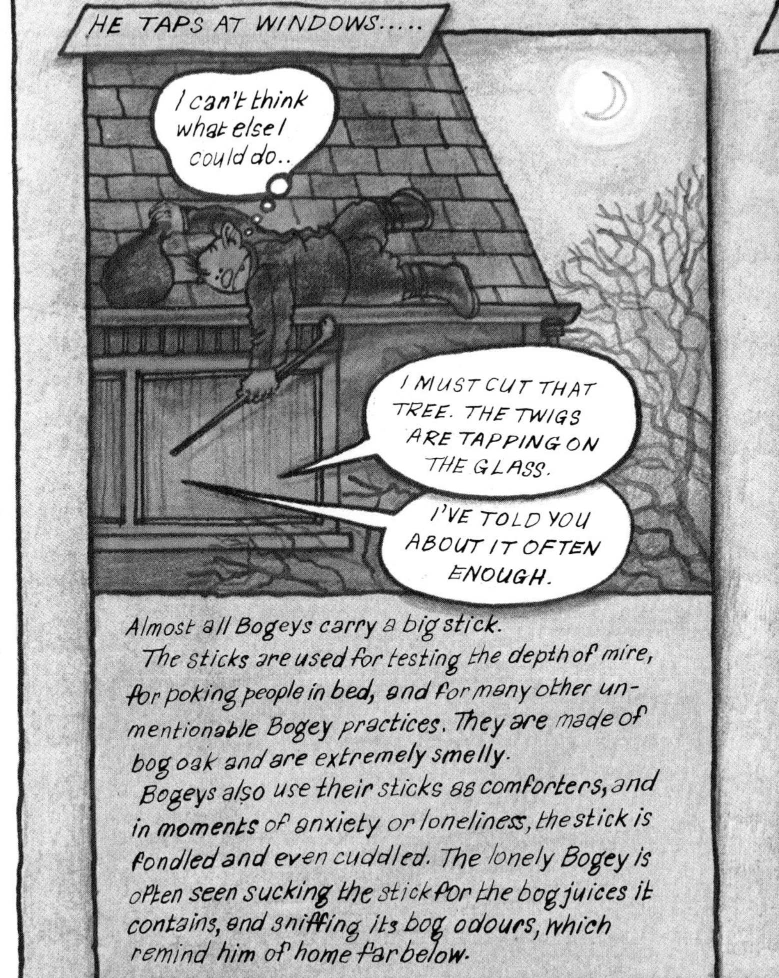
HE TAPS AT WINDOWS.....
I can't think what else I could do..
I MUST CUT THAT TREE. THE TWIGS ARE TAPPING ON THE GLASS.
I'VE TOLD YOU ABOUT IT OFTEN ENOUGH.

Almost all Bogeys carry a big stick.

The sticks are used for testing the depth of mire, for poking people in bed, and for many other unmentionable Bogey practices. They are made of bog oak and are extremely smelly.

Bogeys also use their sticks as comforters, and in moments of anxiety or loneliness, the stick is fondled and even cuddled. The lonely Bogey is often seen sucking the stick for the bog juices it contains, and sniffing its bog odours, which remind him of home far below.

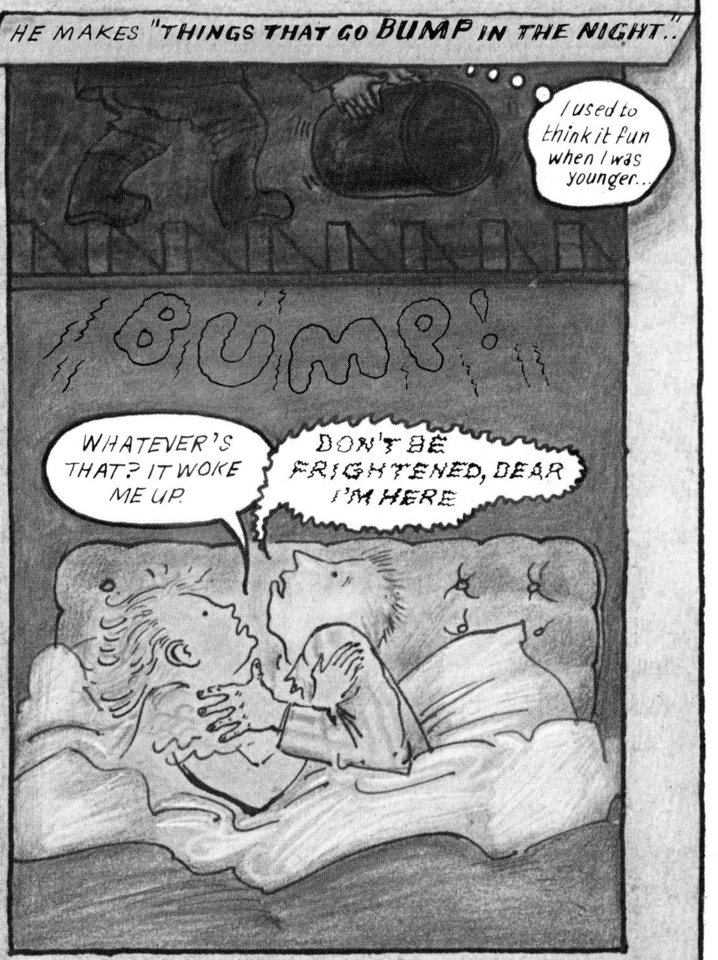
HE MAKES "THINGS THAT GO BUMP IN THE NIGHT"..
I used to think it fun when I was younger...
BUMP!
WHATEVER'S THAT? IT WOKE ME UP.
DON'T BE FRIGHTENED, DEAR I'M HERE

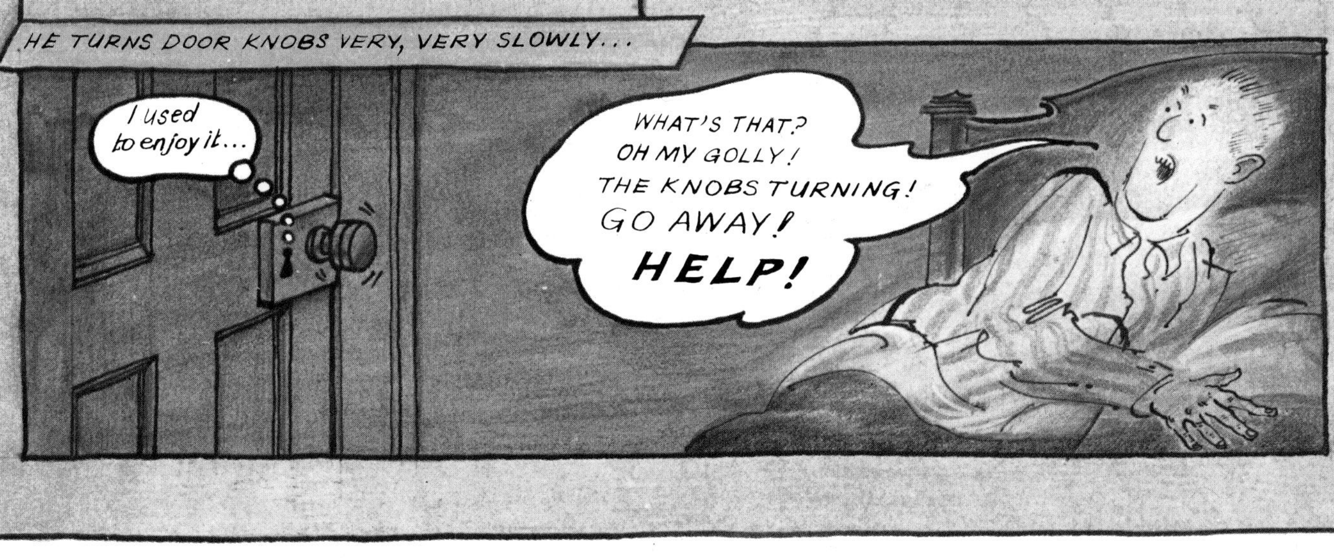
HE TURNS DOOR KNOBS VERY, VERY SLOWLY...
I used to enjoy it...
WHAT'S THAT? OH MY GOLLY! THE KNOBS TURNING! GO AWAY! HELP!

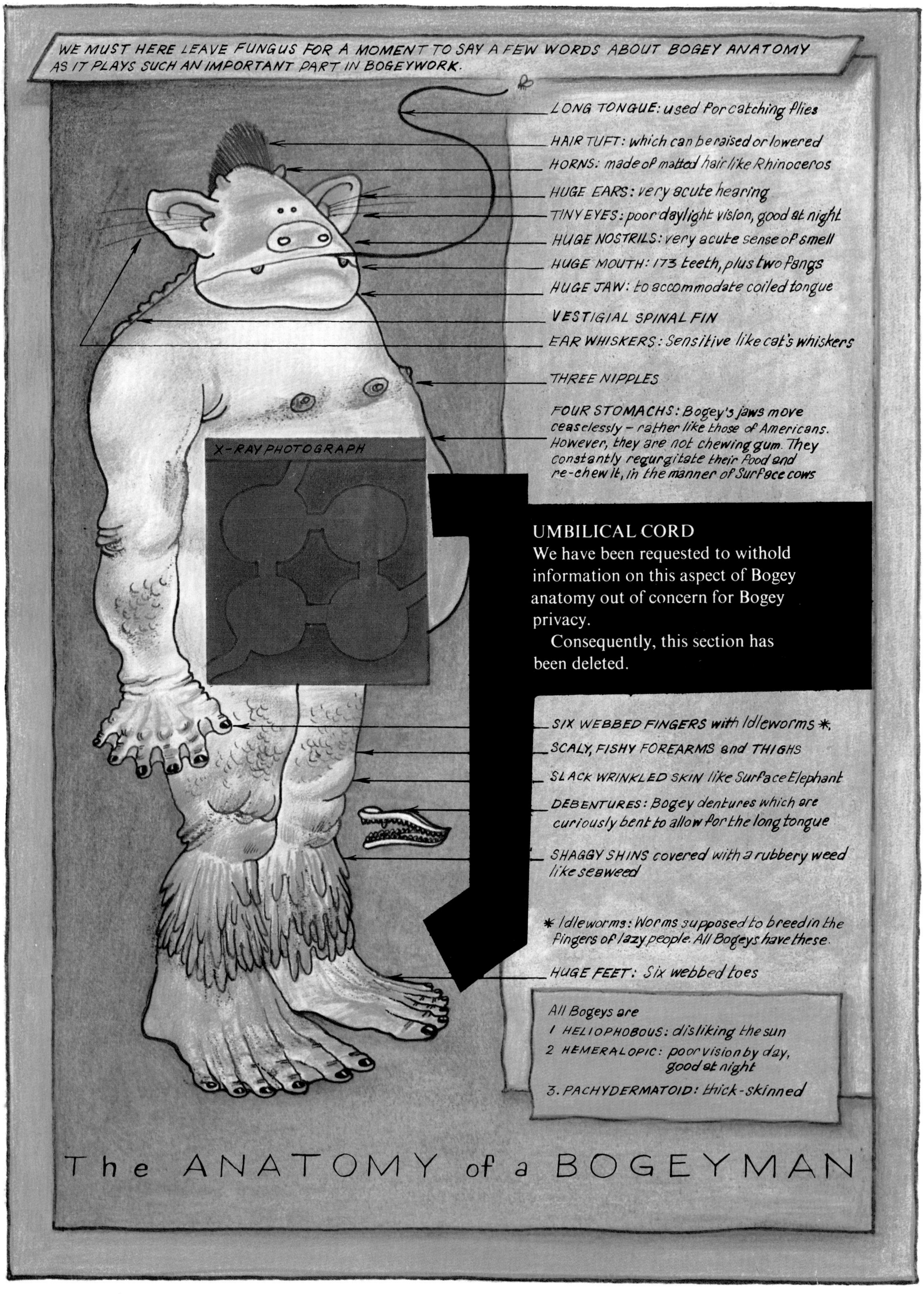
WE MUST HERE LEAVE FUNGUS FOR A MOMENT TO SAY A FEW WORDS ABOUT BOGEY ANATOMY AS IT PLAYS SUCH AN IMPORTANT PART IN BOGEYWORK.
LONG TONGUE: used for catching flies
HAIR TUFT: which can be raised or lowered
HORNS: made of matted hair like Rhinoceros
HUGE EARS: very acute hearing
TINY EYES: poor daylight vision, good at night
HUGE NOSTRILS: very acute sense of smell
HUGE MOUTH: 173 teeth, plus two fangs
HUGE JAW: to accommodate coiled tongue
VESTIGIAL SPINAL FIN
EAR WHISKERS: Sensitive like cat's whiskers
THREE NIPPLES
FOUR STOMACHS: Bogey's jaws move ceaselessly – rather like those of Americans. However, they are not chewing gum. They constantly regurgitate their food and re-chew it, in the manner of Surface cows
X-RAY PHOTOGRAPH
UMBILICAL CORD
We have been requested to withold information on this aspect of Bogey anatomy out of concern for Bogey privacy.
Consequently, this section has been deleted.
SIX WEBBED FINGERS with Idleworms ✱.
SCALY, FISHY FOREARMS and THIGHS
SLACK WRINKLED SKIN like Surface Elephant
DEBENTURES: Bogey dentures which are curiously bent to allow for the long tongue
SHAGGY SHINS covered with a rubbery weed like seaweed
✱ Idleworms: Worms supposed to breed in the fingers of lazy people. All Bogeys have these.
HUGE FEET: Six webbed toes
All Bogeys are
1 HELIOPHOBOUS: disliking the sun
2 HEMERALOPIC: poor vision by day, good at night
3. PACHYDERMATOID: thick-skinned
The ANATOMY of a BOGEYMAN

Bogey anatomy is adapted to wetness and cold. To survive in the dryness and warmth of The Surface, Bogeymen occasionally need special CLOTHING and EQUIPMENT

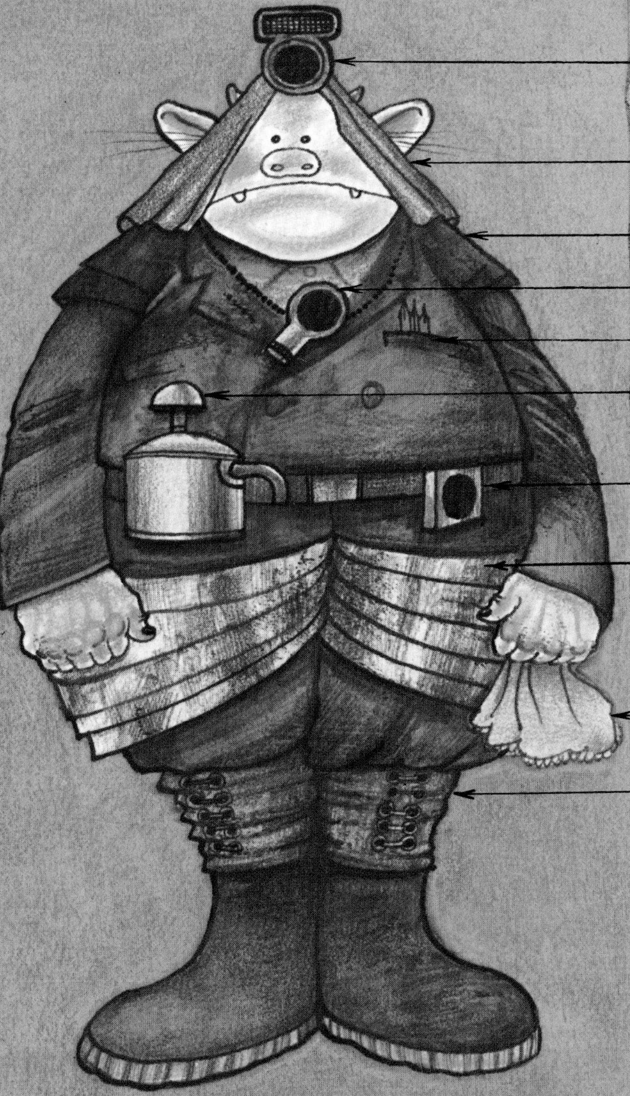

KONISCOPE: An instrument for indicating the amount of dust in the atmosphere. Bogeymen are allergic to dust, pollen and all other manifestations of dryness

LAMBREQUIN or HAVELOCK: a light covering worn over the head and neck as a protection against moonstroke

STERCORACEOUS * DUNGAREES

DROSOMETER: An instrument for measuring the quantity of dew falling on a body during the night

KEELIVINES: Lead-pencils

IMPERMEATOR: a contrivance for lubricating the interior surfaces of a Bogeyman's trousers by the pumping in of oily slime

DASYMETER: an instrument for measuring the density of gases (or smells)

LAMBOYS: A kilted skirt of rusty metal plates, now very old-fashioned and worn only by elderly Bogeymen. Its purpose is to direct valuable evaporations which may have escaped the gennets (q.v.) back to the Bogeyman's vital parts

FOGLE: handkerchief. Bogeymen retain the English 18th century term for these – MUCKENDER

GENICULATES: Bogey knee-bags, popularly known as GENNETS. These protect the knees (as Bogeywork entails a hantle * of kneeling and crawling), but their main purpose is to seal off the boot tops and prevent the evaporation of precious fluids and smells. They also help to prevent GONAGRA (gout in the knee). GENIPAP is the name given to the muck found in the gennets after a night's work. It has an orange colour and a vinous taste

* STERCORACEOUS: pertaining to, or composed of dung

* hantle: a good deal

It sometimes happens that a Bogeyman finds himself unable to reach a Bogeyhole before daylight. If he cannot find a cool, dark hiding place, he will bury himself in a shady spot. In this manner he will evade the heat of the sun and preserve his vital wetness. He will then sleep till darkness falls again.

It is during this time that his projecting hair tuft and ears are sometimes mistaken for a plant. This "plant" was said by the ancients to have a root resembling the human form and to shriek when pulled up; and it is this that lies behind the legend of the Mandragora or MANDRAKE.

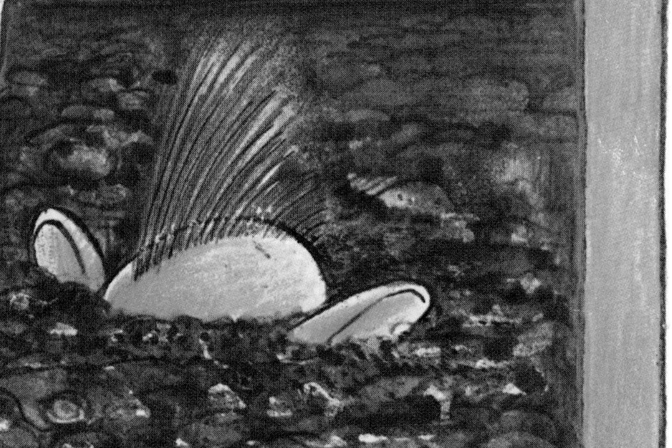

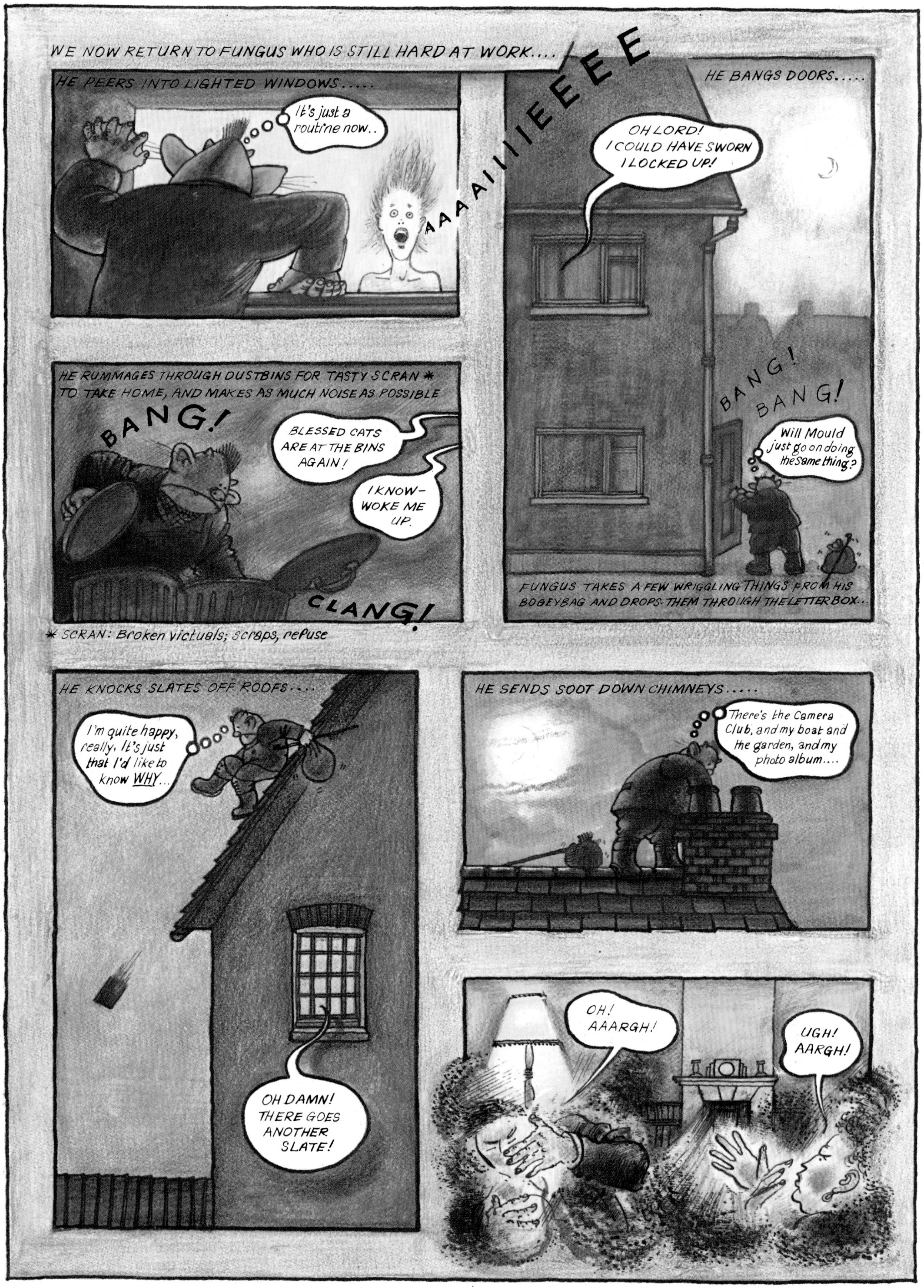
WE NOW RETURN TO FUNGUS WHO IS STILL HARD AT WORK....
HE PEERS INTO LIGHTED WINDOWS.....
It's just a routine now..
AAAAIIIIEEEEE
HE BANGS DOORS.....
OH LORD! I COULD HAVE SWORN I LOCKED UP!
HE RUMMAGES THROUGH DUSTBINS FOR TASTY SCRAN * TO TAKE HOME, AND MAKES AS MUCH NOISE AS POSSIBLE
BANG!
BLESSED CATS ARE AT THE BINS AGAIN!
I KNOW- WOKE ME UP.
CLANG!
BANG! BANG!
Will Mould just go on doing the same thing?
FUNGUS TAKES A FEW WRIGGLING THINGS FROM HIS BOGEYBAG AND DROPS THEM THROUGH THE LETTER BOX...
* SCRAN: Broken victuals; scraps, refuse
HE KNOCKS SLATES OFF ROOFS....
I'm quite happy, really. It's just that I'd like to know WHY...
OH DAMN! THERE GOES ANOTHER SLATE!
HE SENDS SOOT DOWN CHIMNEYS.....
There's the Camera Club, and my boat and the garden, and my photo album....
OH! AAARGH!
UGH! AARGH!

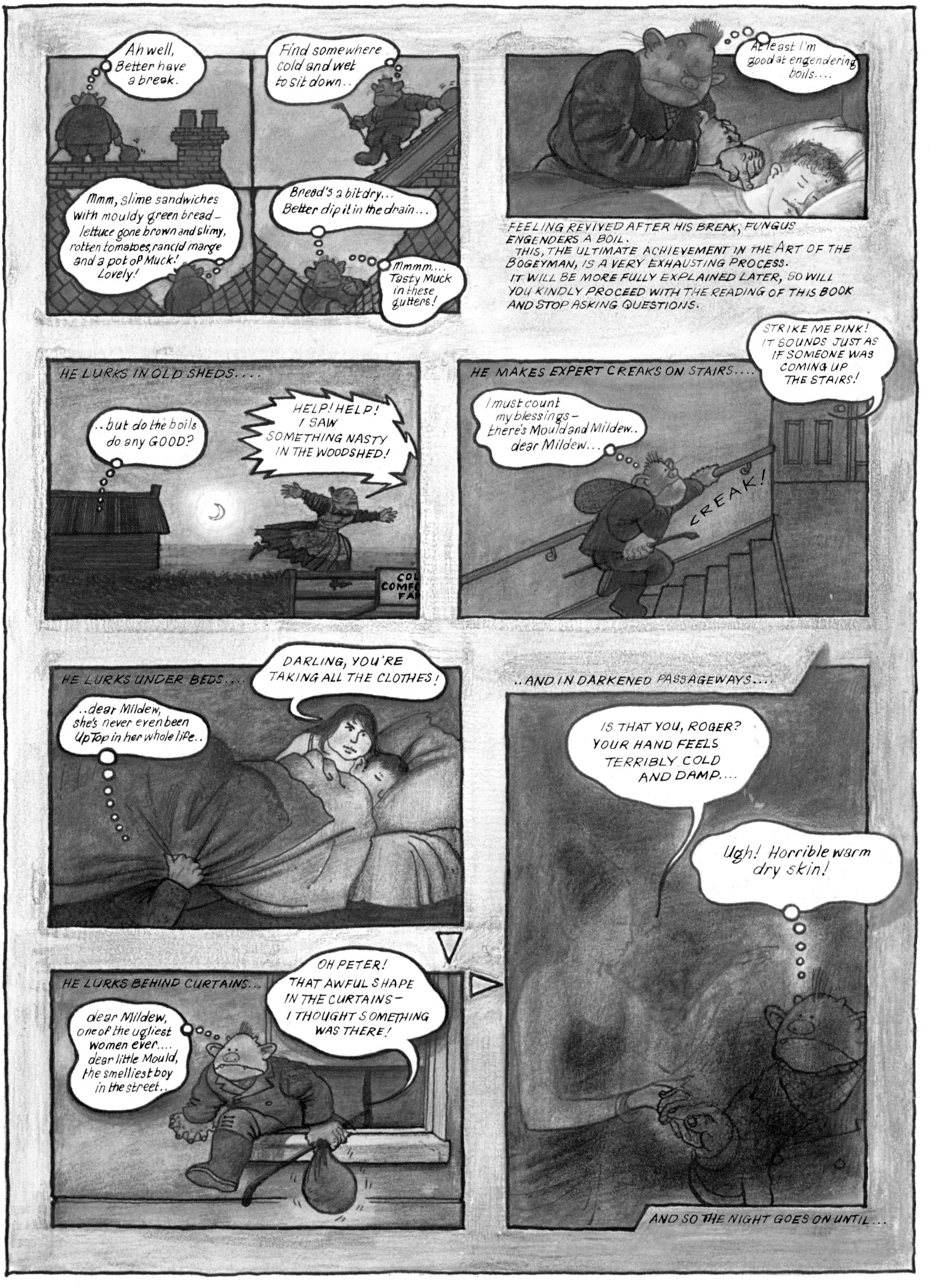

Ah well, Better have a break.
Find somewhere cold and wet to sit down..
Mmm, slime sandwiches with mouldy green bread - lettuce gone brown and slimy, rotten tomatoes, rancid marge and a pot of Muck! Lovely!
Bread's a bit dry... Better dip it in the drain...
Mmmm.... Tasty Muck in these gutters!
At least I'm good at engendering boils....
FEELING REVIVED AFTER HIS BREAK, FUNGUS ENGENDERS A BOIL.
THIS, THE ULTIMATE ACHIEVEMENT IN THE ART OF THE BOGEYMAN, IS A VERY EXHAUSTING PROCESS.
IT WILL BE MORE FULLY EXPLAINED LATER, SO WILL YOU KINDLY PROCEED WITH THE READING OF THIS BOOK AND STOP ASKING QUESTIONS.
HE LURKS IN OLD SHEDS....
..but do the boils do any GOOD?
HELP! HELP! I SAW SOMETHING NASTY IN THE WOODSHED!
HE MAKES EXPERT CREAKS ON STAIRS....
STRIKE ME PINK! IT SOUNDS JUST AS IF SOMEONE WAS COMING UP THE STAIRS!
I must count my blessings - there's Mould and Mildew.. dear Mildew...
CREAK!
HE LURKS UNDER BEDS....
DARLING, YOU'RE TAKING ALL THE CLOTHES!
..dear Mildew, she's never even been Up Top in her whole life..
HE LURKS BEHIND CURTAINS...
OH PETER! THAT AWFUL SHAPE IN THE CURTAINS - I THOUGHT SOMETHING WAS THERE!
dear Mildew, one of the ugliest women ever.... dear little Mould, the smelliest boy in the street..
..AND IN DARKENED PASSAGEWAYS....
IS THAT YOU, ROGER? YOUR HAND FEELS TERRIBLY COLD AND DAMP....
Ugh! Horrible warm dry skin!
AND SO THE NIGHT GOES ON UNTIL...

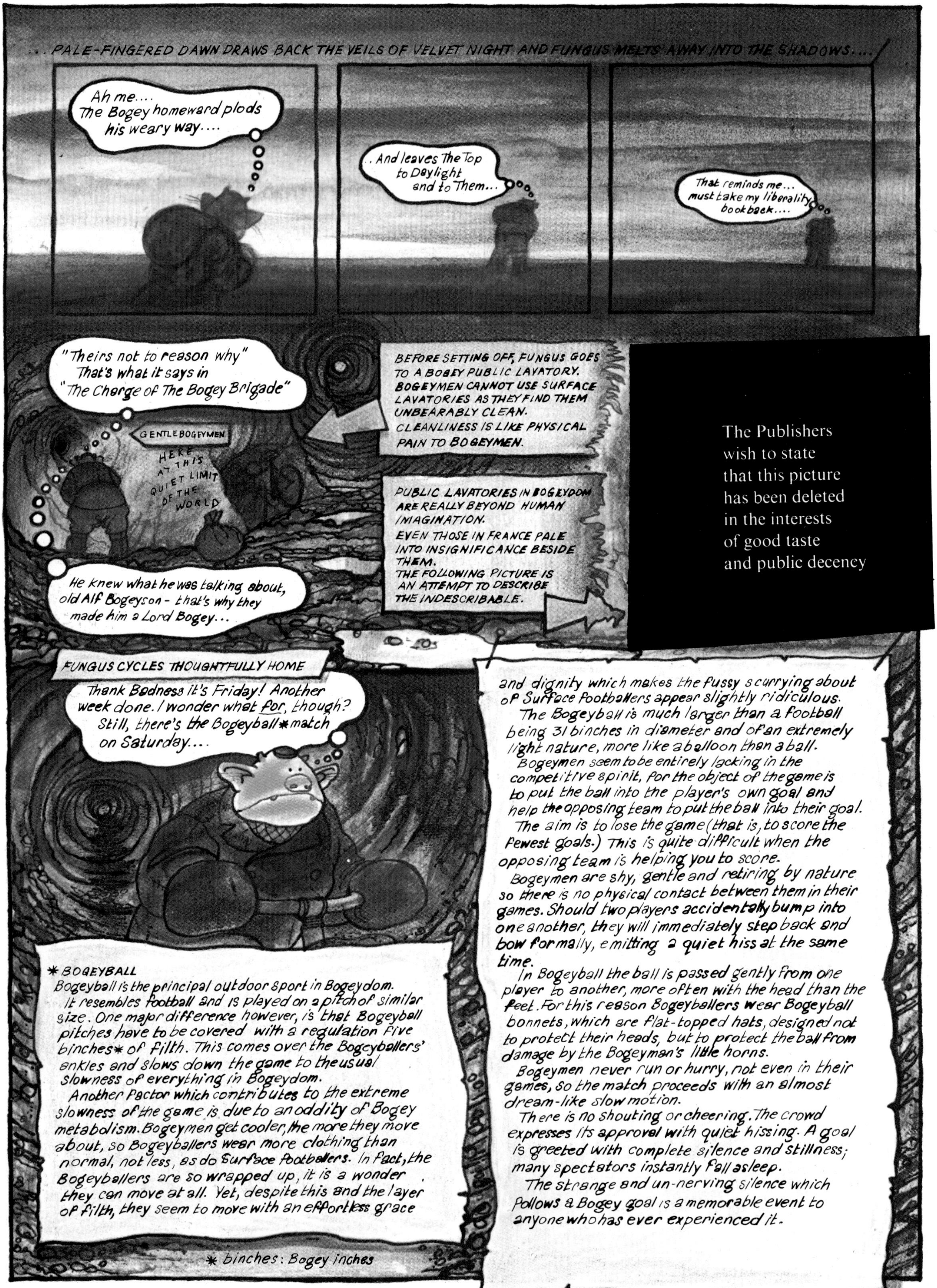

. . . PALE-FINGERED DAWN DRAWS BACK THE VEILS OF VELVET NIGHT AND FUNGUS MELTS AWAY INTO THE SHADOWS . . . .
Ah me.... The Bogey homeward plods his weary way....
. . And leaves The Top to Daylight and to Them...
That reminds me... must take my liberality book back....
"Theirs not to reason why" That's what it says in "The Charge of The Bogey Brigade"
GENTLE BOGEYMEN
HERE AT THIS QUIET LIMIT OF THE WORLD
He knew what he was talking about, old Alf Bogeyson - that's why they made him a Lord Bogey...
BEFORE SETTING OFF, FUNGUS GOES TO A BOGEY PUBLIC LAVATORY. BOGEYMEN CANNOT USE SURFACE LAVATORIES AS THEY FIND THEM UNBEARABLY CLEAN. CLEANLINESS IS LIKE PHYSICAL PAIN TO BOGEYMEN.
PUBLIC LAVATORIES IN BOGEYDOM ARE REALLY BEYOND HUMAN IMAGINATION. EVEN THOSE IN FRANCE PALE INTO INSIGNIFICANCE BESIDE THEM. THE FOLLOWING PICTURE IS AN ATTEMPT TO DESCRIBE THE INDESCRIBABLE.
The Publishers wish to state that this picture has been deleted in the interests of good taste and public decency
FUNGUS CYCLES THOUGHTFULLY HOME
Thank Badness it's Friday! Another week done. I wonder what for, though? Still, there's the Bogeyball✱ match on Saturday....
✱ BOGEYBALL
Bogeyball is the principal outdoor sport in Bogeydom. It resembles football and is played on a pitch of similar size. One major difference however, is that Bogeyball pitches have to be covered with a regulation five binches✱ of filth. This comes over the Bogeyballers' ankles and slows down the game to the usual slowness of everything in Bogeydom.
Another factor which contributes to the extreme slowness of the game is due to an oddity of Bogey metabolism. Bogeymen get cooler, the more they move about, so Bogeyballers wear more clothing than normal, not less, as do Surface footballers. In fact, the Bogeyballers are so wrapped up, it is a wonder they can move at all. Yet, despite this and the layer of filth, they seem to move with an effortless grace and dignity which makes the fussy scurrying about of Surface footballers appear slightly ridiculous.
The Bogeyball is much larger than a football being 31 binches in diameter and of an extremely light nature, more like a balloon than a ball.
Bogeymen seem to be entirely lacking in the competitive spirit, for the object of the game is to put the ball into the player's own goal and help the opposing team to put the ball into their goal.
The aim is to lose the game (that is, to score the fewest goals.) This is quite difficult when the opposing team is helping you to score.
Bogeymen are shy, gentle and retiring by nature so there is no physical contact between them in their games. Should two players accidentally bump into one another, they will immediately step back and bow formally, emitting a quiet hiss at the same time.
In Bogeyball the ball is passed gently from one player to another, more often with the head than the feet. For this reason Bogeyballers wear Bogeyball bonnets, which are flat-topped hats, designed not to protect their heads, but to protect the ball from damage by the Bogeyman's little horns.
Bogeymen never run or hurry, not even in their games, so the match proceeds with an almost dream-like slow motion.
There is no shouting or cheering. The crowd expresses its approval with quiet hissing. A goal is greeted with complete silence and stillness; many spectators instantly fall asleep.
The strange and un-nerving silence which follows a Bogey goal is a memorable event to anyone who has ever experienced it.
✱ binches: Bogey inches

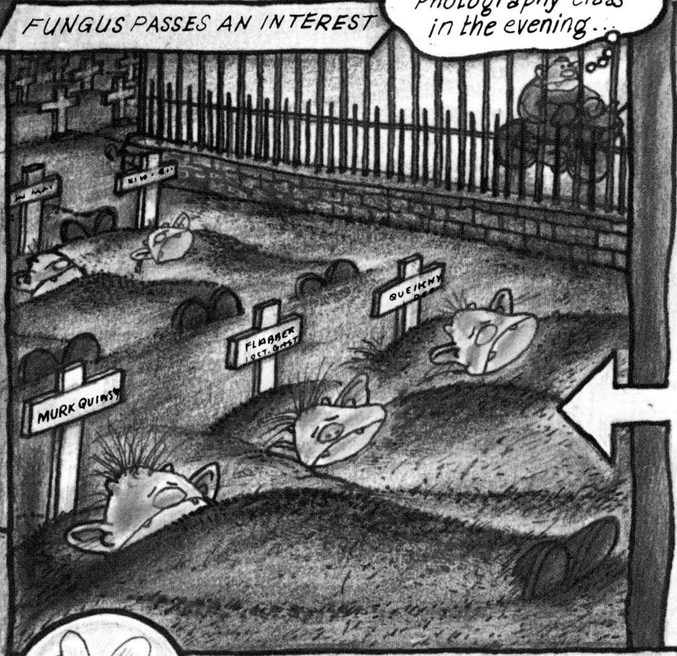
FUNGUS PASSES AN INTEREST
Photography class in the evening...

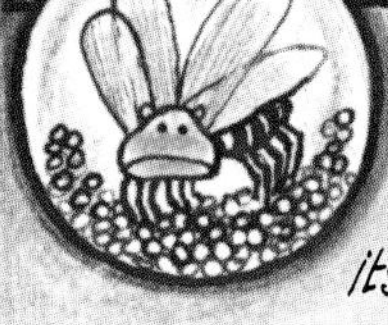

INTERSECT: A species of Bogey Fly which inhabits the Interests and causes a degree of nuisance by laying its eggs in the sleepers' nostrils. Few Bogeys seem to object, however, and on awakening merely sniff up the maggots like snuff, or blow them downwards onto their tongue and eat them.

INTERESTS

There are many Interests in Bogeydom. It is here that Bogeys go whenever they are tired, bored or oppressed by worries. They are then interred by the Interns and sleep for as long as they like, (up to a limit of one year.) No one, not even a close relation, is allowed to waken them for any reason whatsoever. Many painful problems are avoided in this manner and it may account for Bogey longevity. When the sleeper awakes, the problem has receded so far into the past it might never have existed at all.

A one year limit was set as it was found that a longer period caused psychological and social problems of re-adjustment. After two or more years some dis-orientation was observed.

Bogeys can live off the fat of their bodies in the same way as hibernating Surface animals. Apart from a sprinkling of water in dry weather, the sleepers require no attention at all.

The crosses are simply labels with the Bogey's name and date for awakening.

BOGEY PHOTOGRAPHY

It is surprising how many Bogeys are keen photographers in view of the darkness and dirt of the Bogey world. Photography is an art which demands light and cleanliness, perhaps more than any other.

However, Bogeymen are to be seen everywhere with their waterproof cameras, which have huge lenses to cope with the inadequate light of Bogeydom.

The results, judged by Surface standards, are not inspiring. The Bogey's lens is usually filthy, and the film has been put in with twelve dirty, sticky fingers.

The laboratories at BOGAK are choked with dirt and slime, and the films are often mouldy before the Bogey buys them.

The resulting prints, dark to the point of impenetrability, scratched, dirty and mouldy are regarded by Bogeymen with pride and delight.

They are stuck in mildewy albums and proudly shown to visitors.

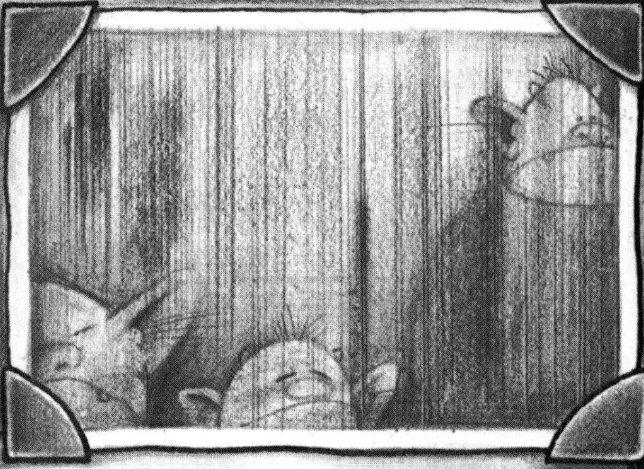

Here we see an unusually fine example of a Bogachome print (19 secs. at f 1·8)

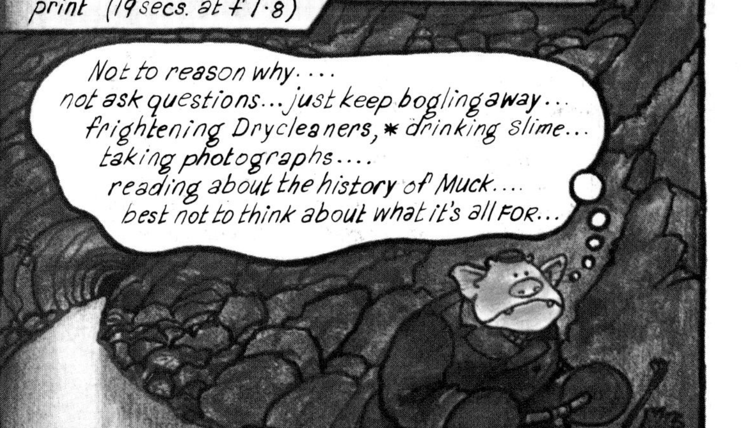
Not to reason why....
not ask questions... just keep bogling away...
frightening Drycleaners, * drinking slime...
taking photographs....
reading about the history of Muck....
best not to think about what it's all FOR...

* Drycleaners: the Surface people

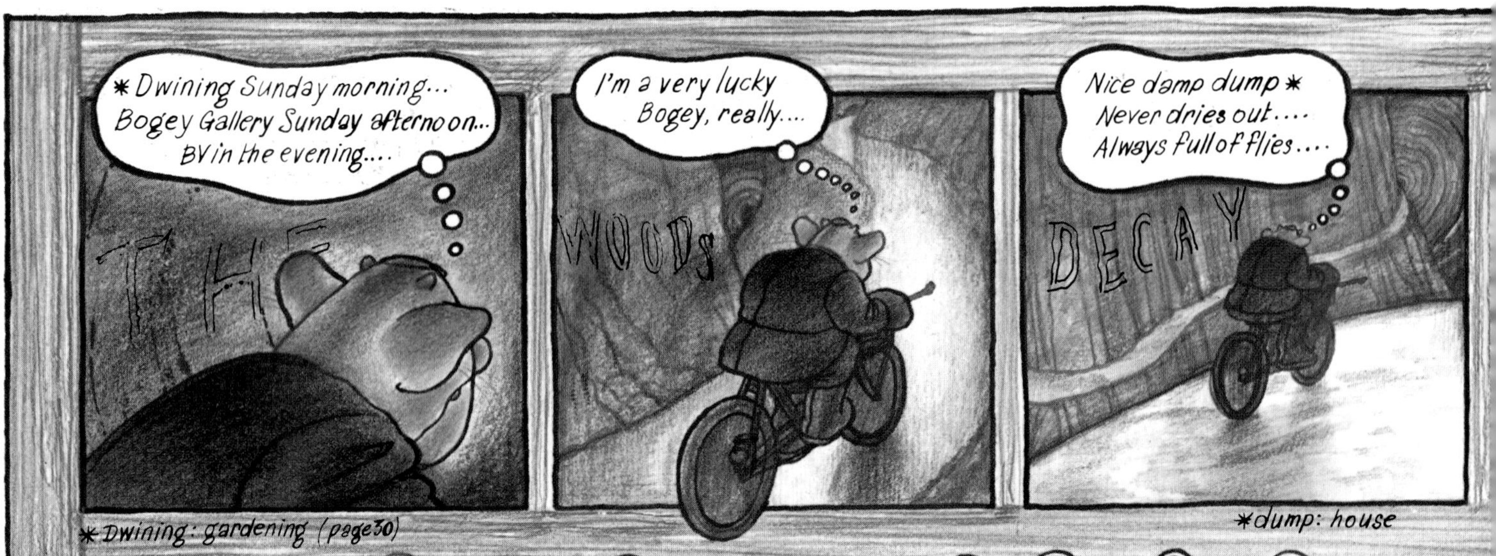
*Dwining Sunday morning…
Bogey Gallery Sunday afternoon…
BV in the evening….
THE
I'm a very lucky
Bogey, really….
WOODS
Nice damp dump*
Never dries out….
Always full of flies….
DECAY
*Dwining: gardening (page 30)
*dump: house

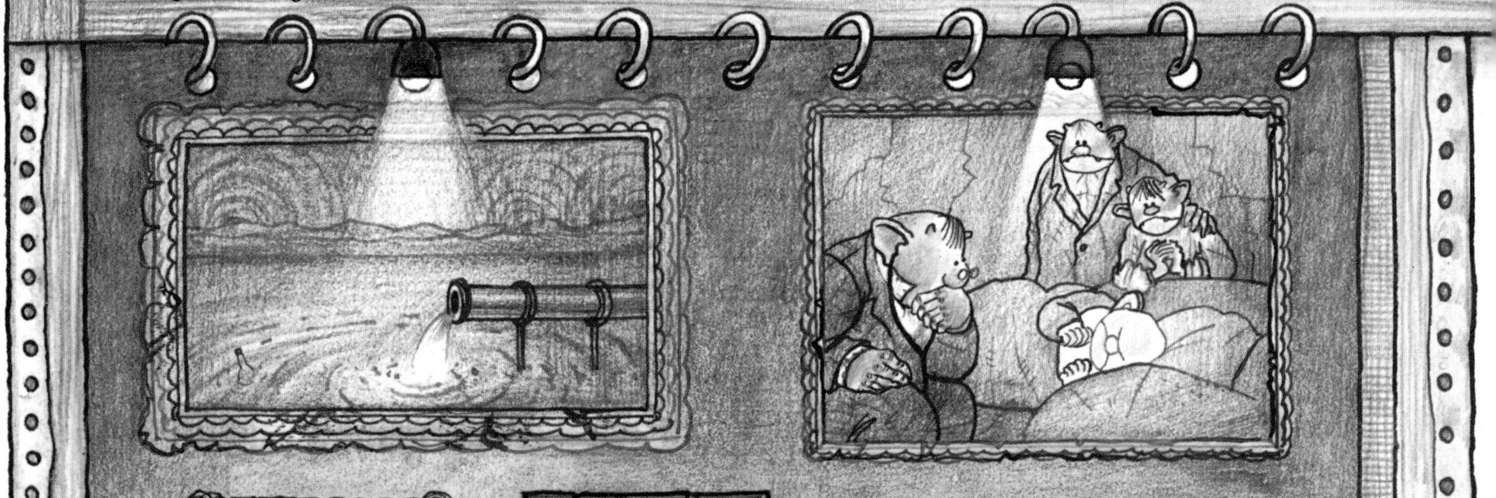

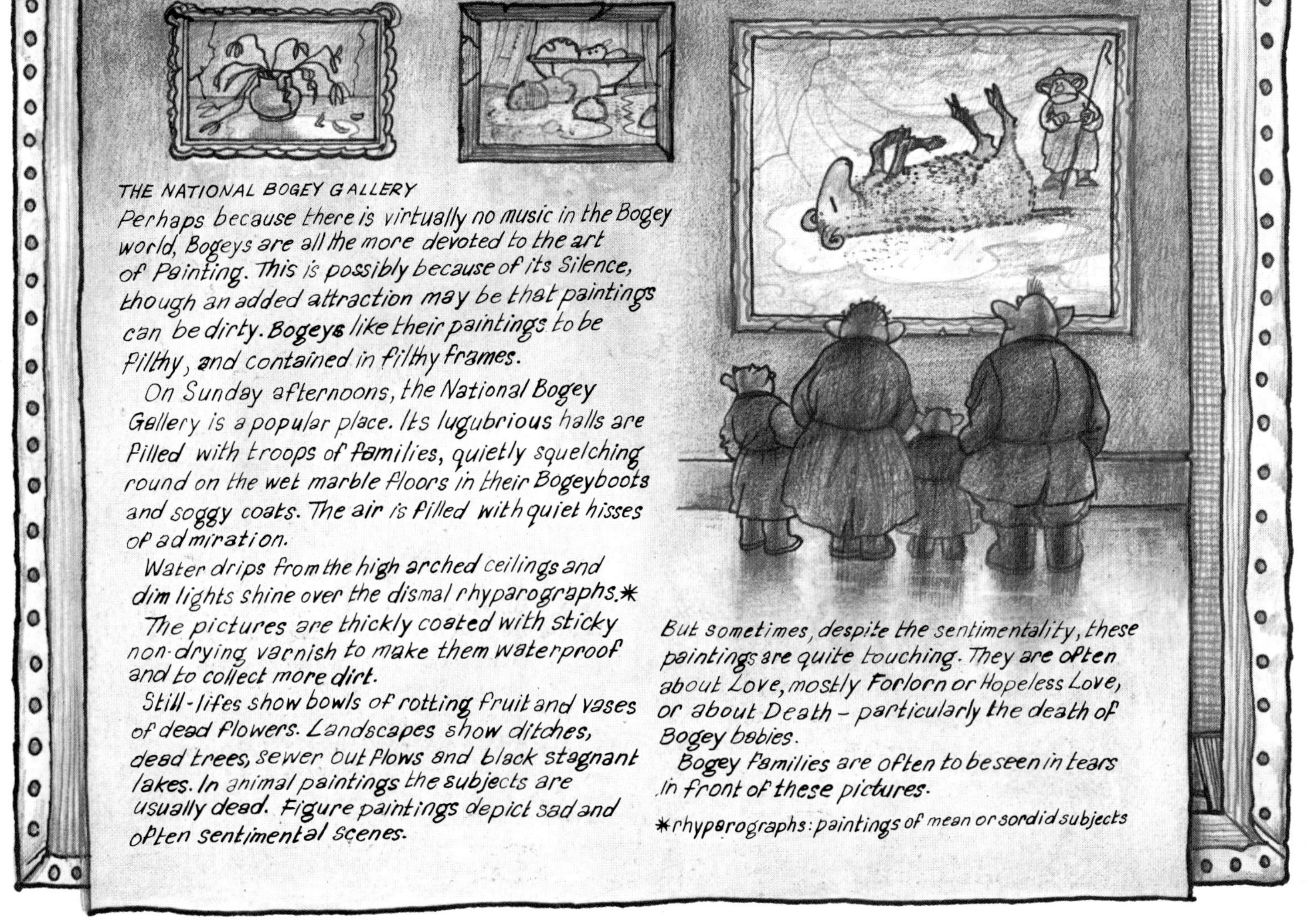

THE NATIONAL BOGEY GALLERY

Perhaps because there is virtually no music in the Bogey world, Bogeys are all the more devoted to the art of Painting. This is possibly because of its Silence, though an added attraction may be that paintings can be dirty. Bogeys like their paintings to be filthy, and contained in filthy frames.

On Sunday afternoons, the National Bogey Gallery is a popular place. Its lugubrious halls are filled with troops of families, quietly squelching round on the wet marble floors in their Bogeyboots and soggy coats. The air is filled with quiet hisses of admiration.

Water drips from the high arched ceilings and dim lights shine over the dismal rhyparographs.*

The pictures are thickly coated with sticky non-drying varnish to make them waterproof and to collect more dirt.

Still-lifes show bowls of rotting fruit and vases of dead flowers. Landscapes show ditches, dead trees, sewer outflows and black stagnant lakes. In animal paintings the subjects are usually dead. Figure paintings depict sad and often sentimental scenes.

But sometimes, despite the sentimentality, these paintings are quite touching. They are often about Love, mostly Forlorn or Hopeless Love, or about Death – particularly the death of Bogey babies.

Bogey families are often to be seen in tears in front of these pictures.

*rhyparographs: paintings of mean or sordid subjects

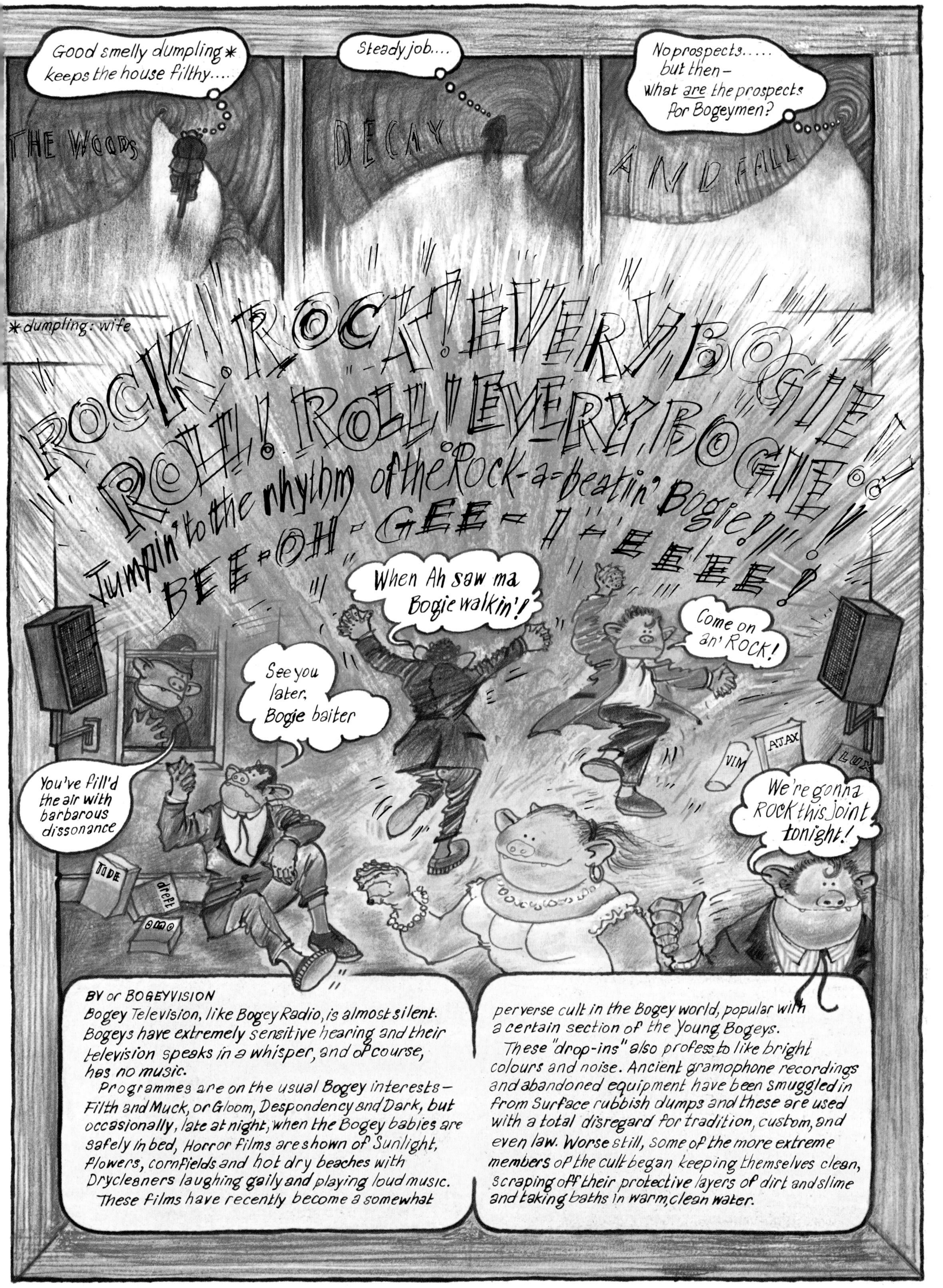
Good smelly dumpling* keeps the house filthy....
Steady job....
No prospects..... but then – What are the prospects for Bogeymen?
THE WOODS
DECAY
AND FALL
*dumpling: wife
ROCK! ROCK! EVERY BOGIE!
ROLL! ROLL! EVERY BOGIE!
Jumpin' to the rhythm of the Rock-a-beatin' Bogie!
BEE-OH-GEE-I-EEEE!
When Ah saw ma Bogie walkin'!
Come on an' ROCK!
See you later, Bogie baiter
You've fill'd the air with barbarous dissonance
We're gonna ROCK this joint tonight!
VIM
AJAX
TIDE
dreft
OMO
BV or BOGEYVISION
Bogey Television, like Bogey Radio, is almost silent. Bogeys have extremely sensitive hearing and their television speaks in a whisper, and of course, has no music.
Programmes are on the usual Bogey interests – Filth and Muck, or Gloom, Despondency and Dark, but occasionally, late at night, when the Bogey babies are safely in bed, Horror films are shown of Sunlight, flowers, cornfields and hot dry beaches with Drycleaners laughing gaily and playing loud music.
These films have recently become a somewhat perverse cult in the Bogey world, popular with a certain section of the Young Bogeys.
These "drop-ins" also profess to like bright colours and noise. Ancient gramophone recordings and abandoned equipment have been smuggled in from Surface rubbish dumps and these are used with a total disregard for tradition, custom, and even law. Worse still, some of the more extreme members of the cult began keeping themselves clean, scraping off their protective layers of dirt and slime and taking baths in warm, clean water.

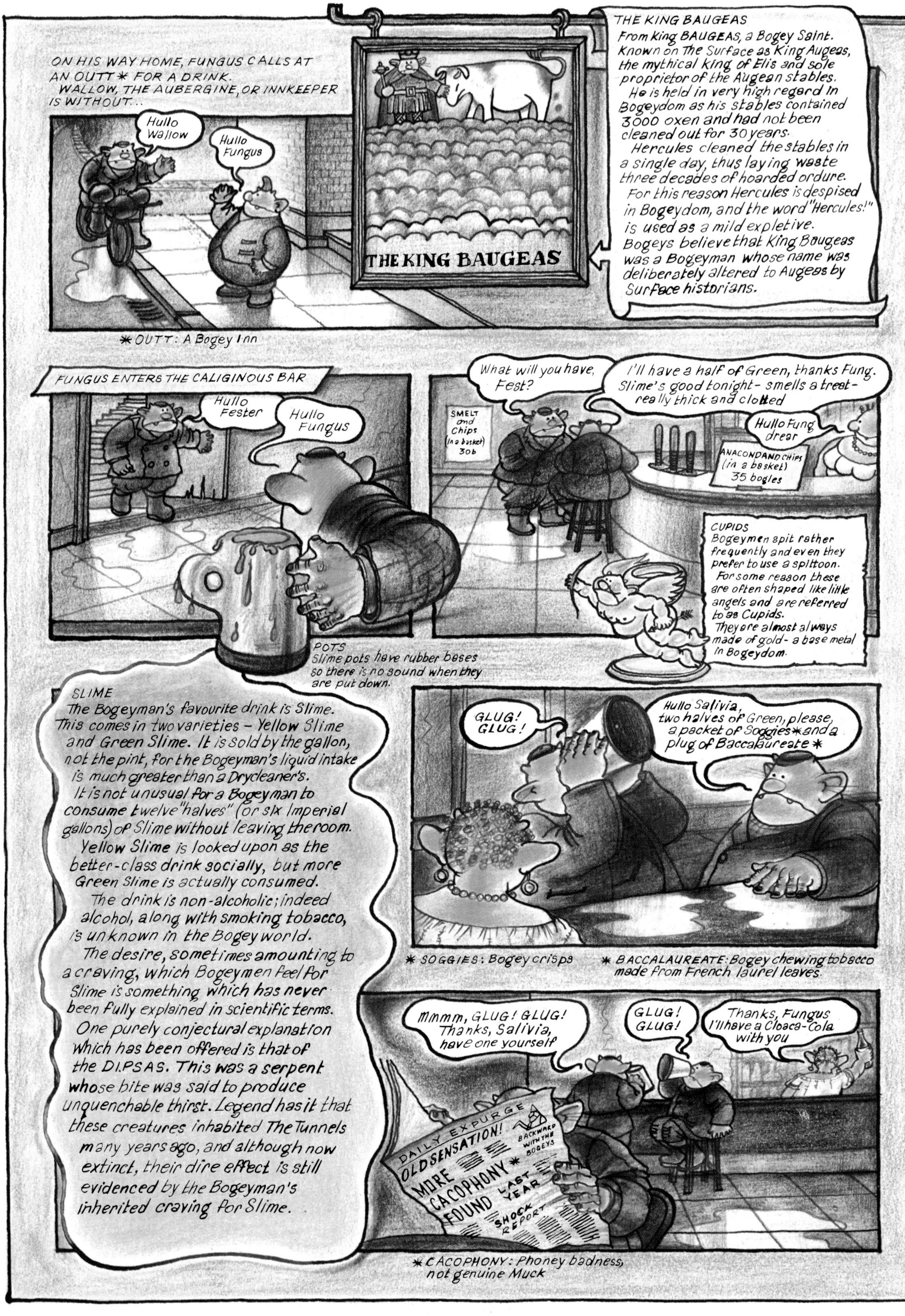
ON HIS WAY HOME, FUNGUS CALLS AT AN OUTT * FOR A DRINK.
WALLOW, THE AUBERGINE, OR INNKEEPER IS WITHOUT...
Hullo Wallow
Hullo Fungus
THE KING BAUGEAS
THE KING BAUGEAS
From King BAUGEAS, a Bogey Saint. Known on The Surface as King Augeas, the mythical king of Elis and sole proprietor of the Augean stables.
He is held in very high regard in Bogeydom as his stables contained 3000 oxen and had not been cleaned out for 30 years.
Hercules cleaned the stables in a single day, thus laying waste three decades of hoarded ordure.
For this reason Hercules is despised in Bogeydom, and the word "Hercules!" is used as a mild expletive.
Bogeys believe that King Baugeas was a Bogeyman whose name was deliberately altered to Augeas by Surface historians.
* OUTT: A Bogey Inn
FUNGUS ENTERS THE CALIGINOUS BAR
Hullo Fester
Hullo Fungus
What will you have, Fest?
I'll have a half of Green, thanks Fung. Slime's good tonight - smells a treat - really thick and clotted
SMELT and Chips (in a basket) 30b
Hullo Fung drear
ANACONDAND CHIPS (in a basket) 35 bogles
CUPIDS
Bogeymen spit rather frequently and even they prefer to use a spittoon.
For some reason these are often shaped like little angels and are referred to as Cupids.
They are almost always made of gold - a base metal in Bogeydom.
POTS
Slime pots have rubber bases so there is no sound when they are put down.
SLIME
The Bogeyman's favourite drink is Slime. This comes in two varieties – Yellow Slime and Green Slime. It is sold by the gallon, not the pint, for the Bogeyman's liquid intake is much greater than a Drycleaner's.
It is not unusual for a Bogeyman to consume twelve "halves" (or six Imperial gallons) of Slime without leaving the room.
Yellow Slime is looked upon as the better-class drink socially, but more Green Slime is actually consumed.
The drink is non-alcoholic; indeed alcohol, along with smoking tobacco, is unknown in the Bogey world.
The desire, sometimes amounting to a craving, which Bogeymen feel for Slime is something which has never been fully explained in scientific terms.
One purely conjectural explanation which has been offered is that of the DIPSAS. This was a serpent whose bite was said to produce unquenchable thirst. Legend has it that these creatures inhabited The Tunnels many years ago, and although now extinct, their dire effect is still evidenced by the Bogeyman's inherited craving for Slime.
GLUG! GLUG!
Hullo Salivia, two halves of Green, please, a packet of Soggies * and a plug of Baccalaureate *
* SOGGIES: Bogey crisps
* BACCALAUREATE: Bogey chewing tobacco made from French laurel leaves.
Mmmm, GLUG! GLUG! Thanks, Salivia, have one yourself
GLUG! GLUG!
Thanks, Fungus I'll have a Cloaca-Cola with you
DAILY EXPURGE
BACKWARD WITH THE BOGEYS
OLD SENSATION!
MORE CACOPHONY FOUND LAST YEAR
SHOCK REPORT
* CACOPHONY: Phoney badness, not genuine Muck

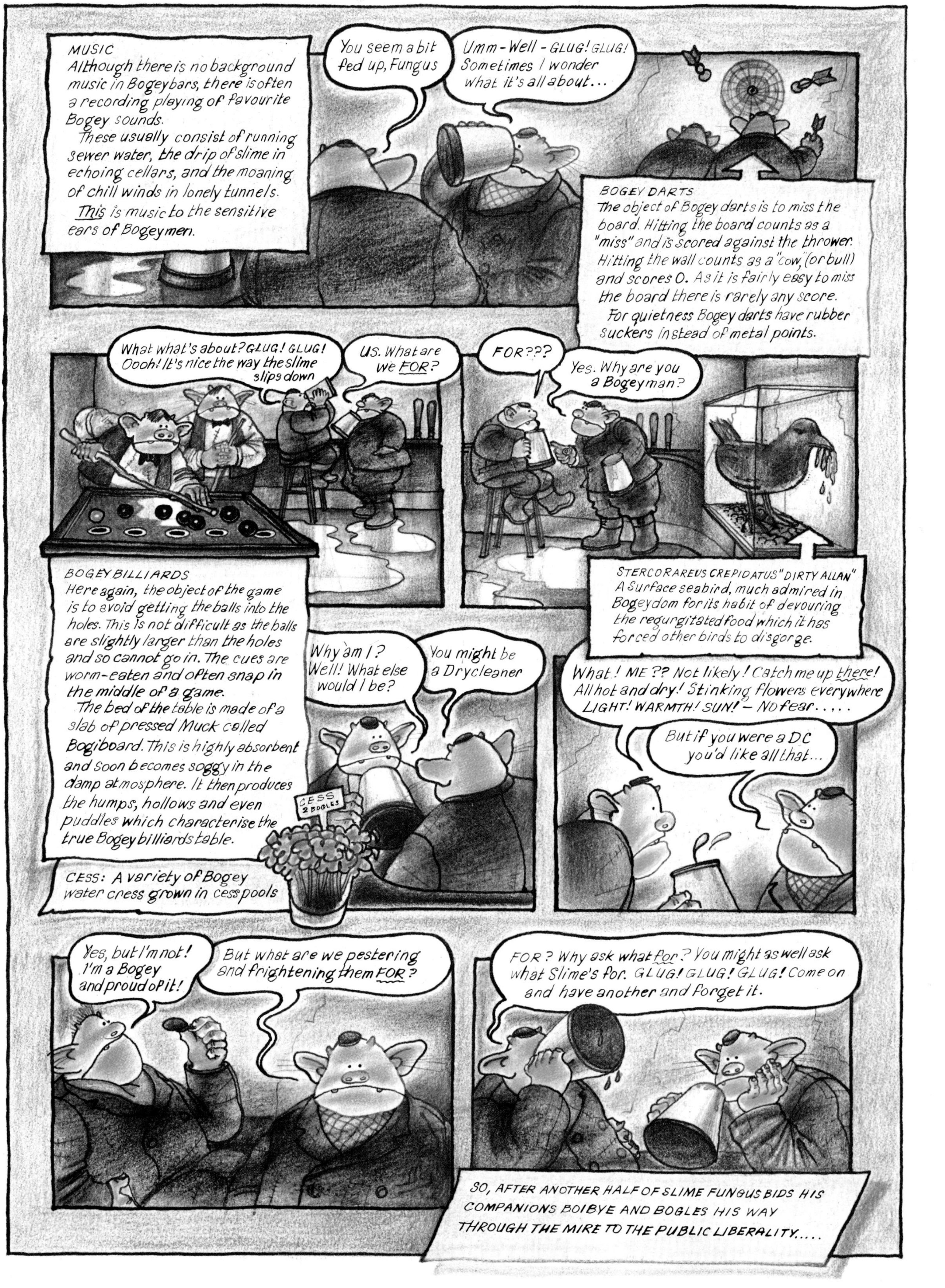
MUSIC
Although there is no background music in Bogeybars, there is often a recording playing of favourite Bogey sounds.
These usually consist of running sewer water, the drip of slime in echoing cellars, and the moaning of chill winds in lonely tunnels.
This is music to the sensitive ears of Bogeymen.
You seem a bit fed up, Fungus
Umm - Well - GLUG! GLUG! Sometimes I wonder what it's all about...
BOGEY DARTS
The object of Bogey darts is to miss the board. Hitting the board counts as a "miss" and is scored against the thrower. Hitting the wall counts as a "cow," (or bull) and scores 0. As it is fairly easy to miss the board there is rarely any score.
For quietness Bogey darts have rubber suckers instead of metal points.
What what's about? GLUG! GLUG! Oooh! It's nice the way the slime slips down
US. What are we FOR?
FOR???
Yes. Why are you a Bogeyman?
BOGEY BILLIARDS
Here again, the object of the game is to avoid getting the balls into the holes. This is not difficult as the balls are slightly larger than the holes and so cannot go in. The cues are worm-eaten and often snap in the middle of a game.
The bed of the table is made of a slab of pressed Muck called Bogiboard. This is highly absorbent and soon becomes soggy in the damp atmosphere. It then produces the humps, hollows and even puddles which characterise the true Bogey billiards table.
STERCORAREUS CREPIDATUS "DIRTY ALLAN"
A Surface seabird, much admired in Bogeydom for its habit of devouring the regurgitated food which it has forced other birds to disgorge.
Why am I? Well! What else would I be?
You might be a Drycleaner
CESS 2 BOGLES
CESS: A variety of Bogey water cress grown in cess pools
What! ME?? Not likely! Catch me up there! All hot and dry! Stinking flowers everywhere LIGHT! WARMTH! SUN! – No fear.....
But if you were a DC you'd like all that...
Yes, but I'm not! I'm a Bogey and proud of it!
But what are we pestering and frightening them FOR?
FOR? Why ask what for? You might as well ask what Slime's for. GLUG! GLUG! GLUG! Come on and have another and forget it.
SO, AFTER ANOTHER HALF OF SLIME FUNGUS BIDS HIS COMPANIONS BOIBYE AND BOGLES HIS WAY THROUGH THE MIRE TO THE PUBLIC LIBERALITY.....

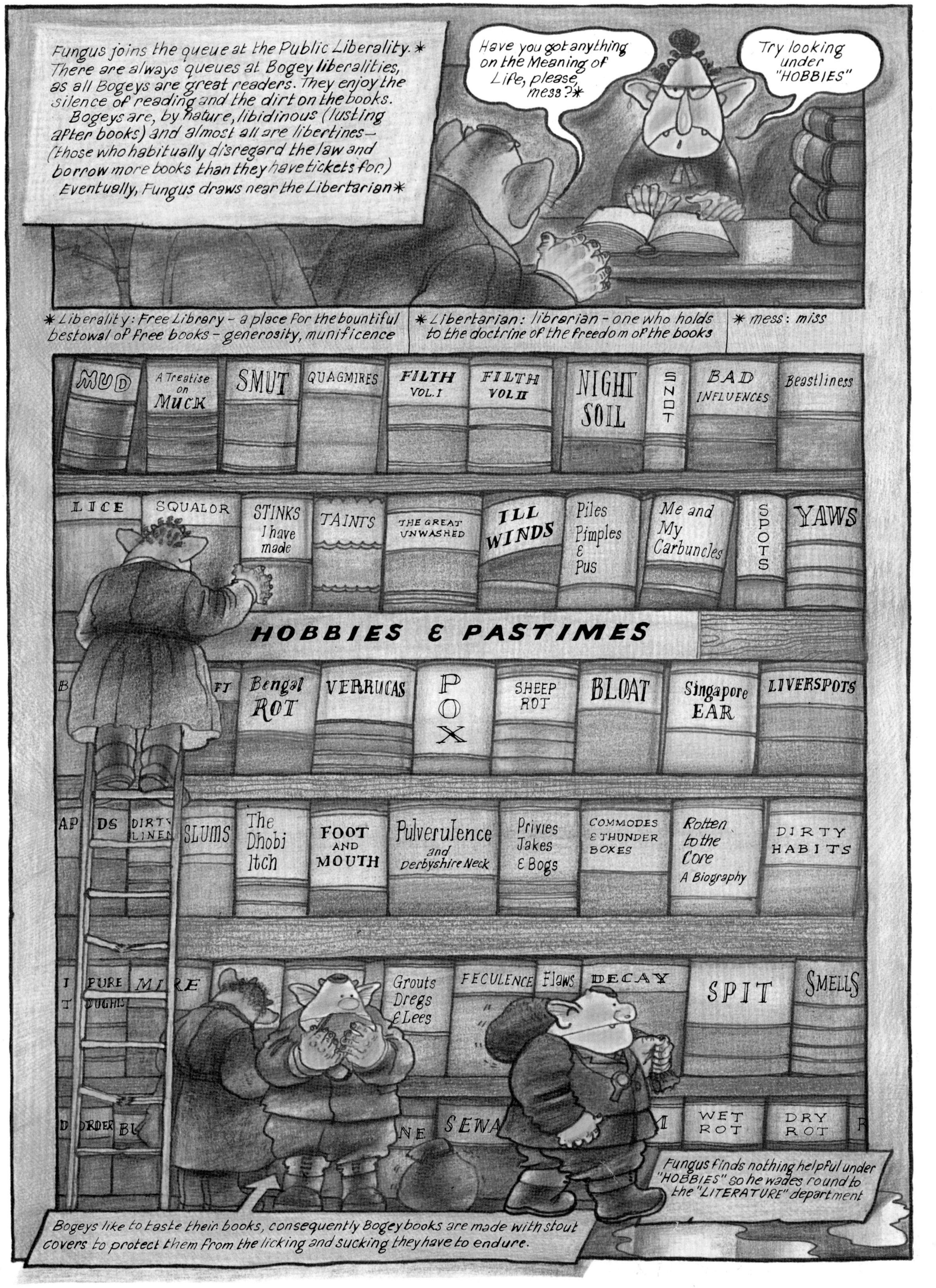
Fungus joins the queue at the Public Liberality.✱ There are always queues at Bogey liberalities, as all Bogeys are great readers. They enjoy the silence of reading and the dirt on the books.
Bogeys are, by nature, libidinous (lusting after books) and almost all are libertines – (those who habitually disregard the law and borrow more books than they have tickets for.)
Eventually, Fungus draws near the Libertarian✱
Have you got anything on the Meaning of Life, please, mess?✱
Try looking under "HOBBIES"
✱ Liberality: Free Library – a place for the bountiful bestowal of free books – generosity, munificence
✱ Libertarian: librarian – one who holds to the doctrine of the freedom of the books
✱ mess: miss
MUD
A Treatise on MUCK
SMUT
QUAGMIRES
FILTH VOL. I
FILTH VOL II
NIGHT SOIL
SNOT
BAD INFLUENCES
Beastliness
LICE
SQUALOR
STINKS I have made
TAINTS
THE GREAT UNWASHED
ILL WINDS
Piles Pimples & Pus
Me and My Carbuncles
SPOTS
YAWS
HOBBIES & PASTIMES
Bengal ROT
VERRUCAS
POX
SHEEP ROT
BLOAT
Singapore EAR
LIVERSPOTS
DIRTY LINEN
SLUMS
The Dhobi Itch
FOOT AND MOUTH
Pulverulence and Derbyshire Neck
Privies Jakes & Bogs
COMMODES & THUNDER BOXES
Rotten to the Core A Biography
DIRTY HABITS
PURE
MIRE
Grouts Dregs & Lees
FECULENCE
Flaws
DECAY
SPIT
SMELLS
WET ROT
DRY ROT
Fungus finds nothing helpful under "HOBBIES" so he wades round to the "LITERATURE" department
Bogeys like to taste their books, consequently Bogey books are made with stout covers to protect them from the licking and sucking they have to endure.

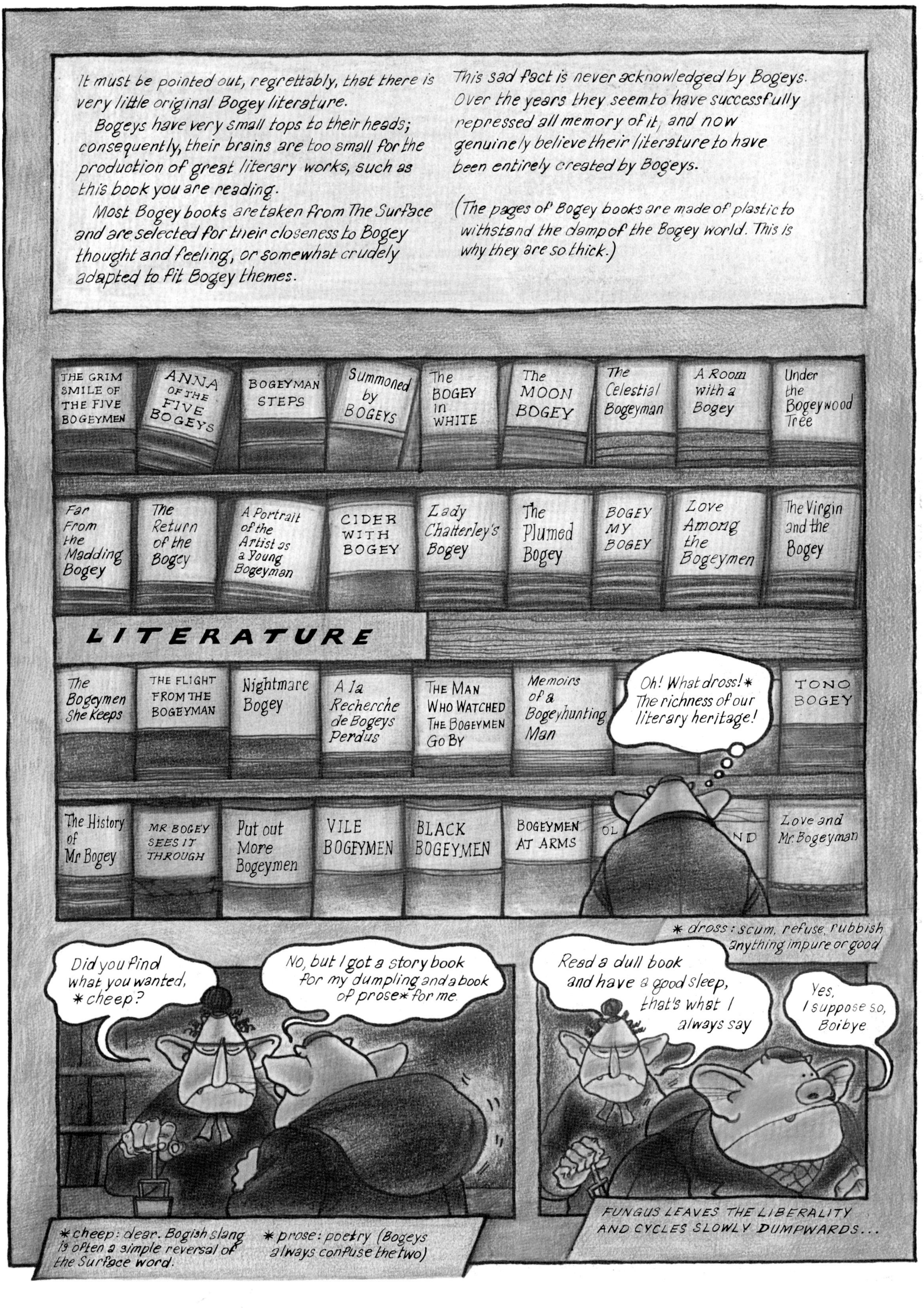
It must be pointed out, regrettably, that there is very little original Bogey literature.
Bogeys have very small tops to their heads; consequently, their brains are too small for the production of great literary works, such as this book you are reading.
Most Bogey books are taken from The Surface and are selected for their closeness to Bogey thought and feeling, or somewhat crudely adapted to fit Bogey themes.
This sad fact is never acknowledged by Bogeys. Over the years they seem to have successfully repressed all memory of it, and now genuinely believe their literature to have been entirely created by Bogeys.
(The pages of Bogey books are made of plastic to withstand the damp of the Bogey world. This is why they are so thick.)
THE GRIM SMILE OF THE FIVE BOGEYMEN
ANNA OF THE FIVE BOGEYS
BOGEYMAN STEPS
Summoned by BOGEYS
The BOGEY in WHITE
The MOON BOGEY
The Celestial Bogeyman
A Room with a Bogey
Under the Bogeywood Tree
Far From the Madding Bogey
The Return of the Bogey
A Portrait of the Artist as a Young Bogeyman
CIDER WITH BOGEY
Lady Chatterley's Bogey
The Plumed Bogey
BOGEY MY BOGEY
Love Among the Bogeymen
The Virgin and the Bogey
LITERATURE
The Bogeymen She Keeps
THE FLIGHT FROM THE BOGEYMAN
Nightmare Bogey
A la Recherche de Bogeys Perdus
THE MAN WHO WATCHED THE BOGEYMEN GO BY
Memoirs of a Bogeyhunting Man
Oh! What dross!* The richness of our literary heritage!
TONO BOGEY
The History of Mr Bogey
MR BOGEY SEES IT THROUGH
Put out More Bogeymen
VILE BOGEYMEN
BLACK BOGEYMEN
BOGEYMEN AT ARMS
Love and Mr Bogeyman
* dross : scum, refuse, rubbish anything impure or good
Did you find what you wanted, *cheep?
No, but I got a story book for my dumpling and a book of prose* for me.
*cheep: dear. Bogish slang is often a simple reversal of the Surface word.
*prose: poetry (Bogeys always confuse the two)
Read a dull book and have a good sleep, that's what I always say
Yes, I suppose so, Boibye
FUNGUS LEAVES THE LIBERALITY AND CYCLES SLOWLY DUMPWARDS...

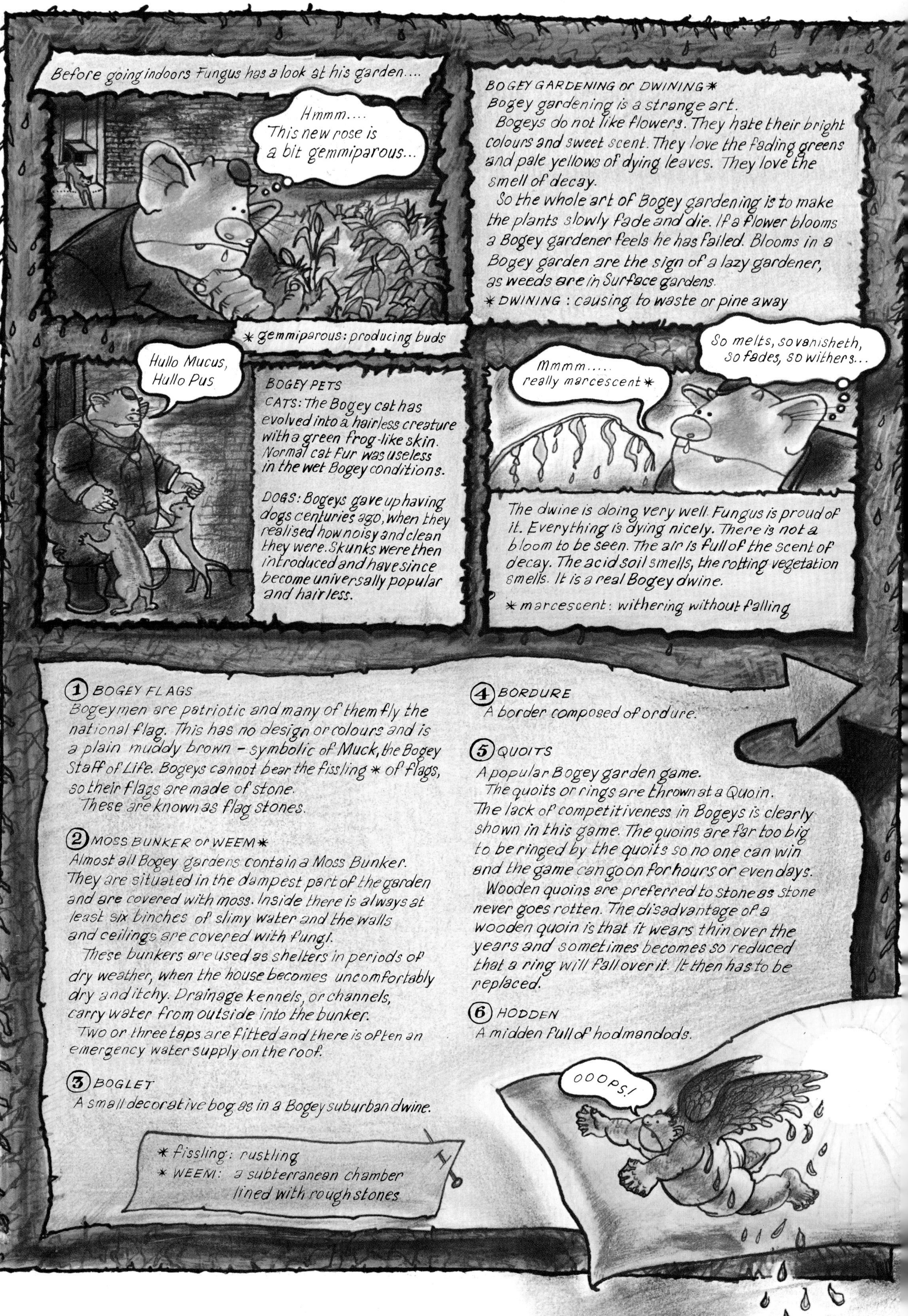
Before going indoors Fungus has a look at his garden....
Hmmm.... This new rose is a bit gemmiparous...
* gemmiparous: producing buds
BOGEY GARDENING OR DWINING*
Bogey gardening is a strange art.
Bogeys do not like flowers. They hate their bright colours and sweet scent. They love the fading greens and pale yellows of dying leaves. They love the smell of decay.
So the whole art of Bogey gardening is to make the plants slowly fade and die. If a flower blooms a Bogey gardener feels he has failed. Blooms in a Bogey garden are the sign of a lazy gardener, as weeds are in Surface gardens.
* DWINING : causing to waste or pine away
Hullo Mucus, Hullo Pus
BOGEY PETS
CATS: The Bogey cat has evolved into a hairless creature with a green frog-like skin. Normal cat fur was useless in the wet Bogey conditions.
DOGS: Bogeys gave up having dogs centuries ago, when they realised how noisy and clean they were. Skunks were then introduced and have since become universally popular and hairless.
Mmmm..... really marcescent*
So melts, so vanisheth, so fades, so withers...
The dwine is doing very well. Fungus is proud of it. Everything is dying nicely. There is not a bloom to be seen. The air is full of the scent of decay. The acid soil smells, the rotting vegetation smells. It is a real Bogey dwine.
* marcescent: withering without falling
1 BOGEY FLAGS
Bogeymen are patriotic and many of them fly the national flag. This has no design or colours and is a plain muddy brown – symbolic of Muck, the Bogey Staff of Life. Bogeys cannot bear the fissling * of flags, so their flags are made of stone.
These are known as flag stones.
2 MOSS BUNKER OR WEEM*
Almost all Bogey gardens contain a Moss Bunker. They are situated in the dampest part of the garden and are covered with moss. Inside there is always at least six binches of slimy water and the walls and ceilings are covered with fungi.
These bunkers are used as shelters in periods of dry weather, when the house becomes uncomfortably dry and itchy. Drainage kennels, or channels, carry water from outside into the bunker.
Two or three taps are fitted and there is often an emergency water supply on the roof.
3 BOGLET
A small decorative bog as in a Bogey suburban dwine.
* fissling: rustling
* WEEM: a subterranean chamber lined with rough stones
4 BORDURE
A border composed of ordure.
5 QUOITS
A popular Bogey garden game.
The quoits or rings are thrown at a Quoin. The lack of competitiveness in Bogeys is clearly shown in this game. The quoins are far too big to be ringed by the quoits so no one can win and the game can go on for hours or even days.
Wooden quoins are preferred to stone as stone never goes rotten. The disadvantage of a wooden quoin is that it wears thin over the years and sometimes becomes so reduced that a ring will fall over it. It then has to be replaced.
6 HODDEN
A midden full of hodmandods.
OOOPS!

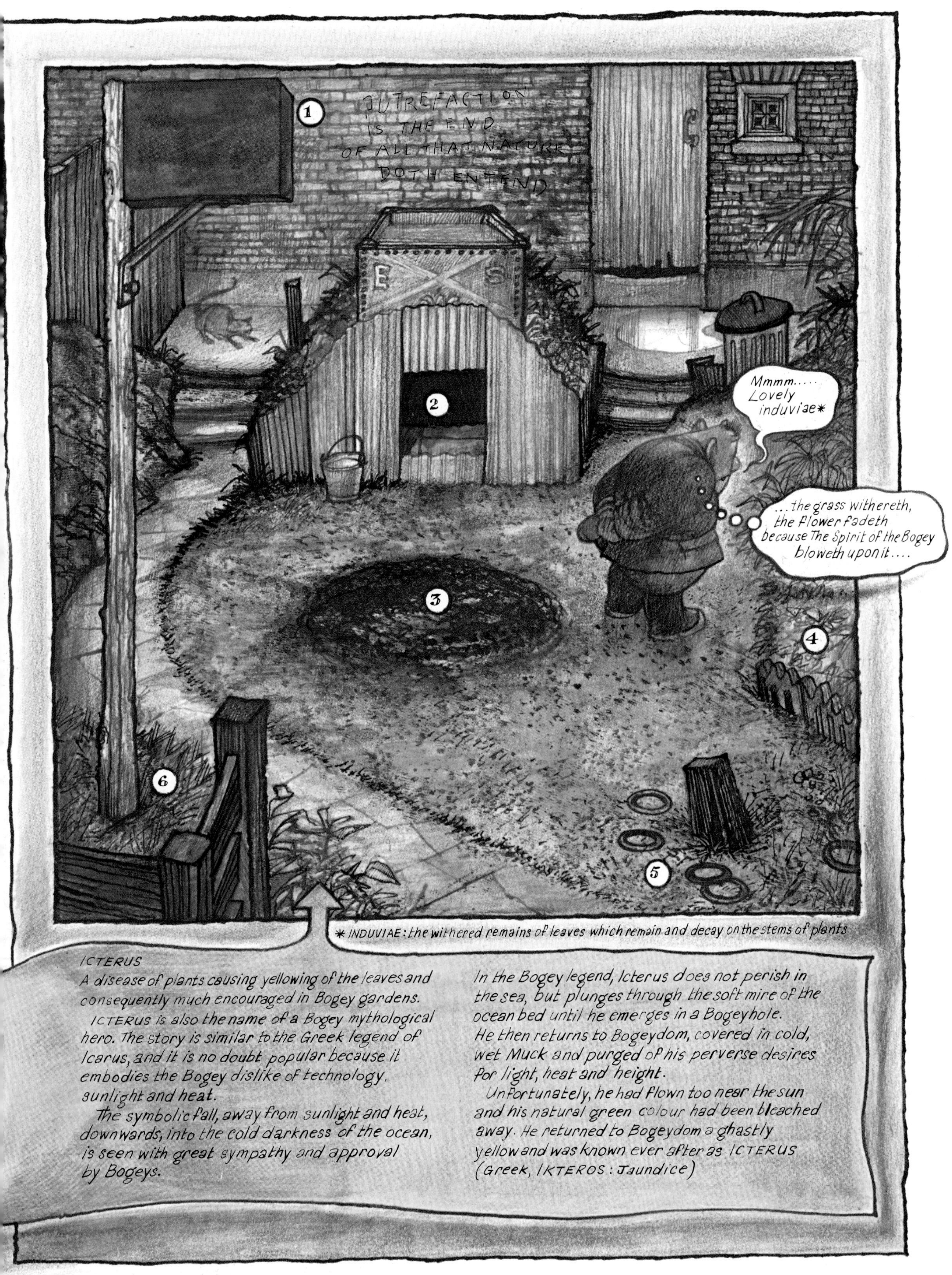
PUTREFACTION IS THE END OF ALL THAT NATURE DOTH ENTEND
1
2
3
4
5
6
Mmmm..... Lovely induviae*
...the grass withereth, the flower fadeth because The Spirit of the Bogey bloweth upon it....

* INDUVIAE: the withered remains of leaves which remain and decay on the stems of plants

ICTERUS

A disease of plants causing yellowing of the leaves and consequently much encouraged in Bogey gardens.

ICTERUS is also the name of a Bogey mythological hero. The story is similar to the Greek legend of Icarus, and it is no doubt popular because it embodies the Bogey dislike of technology, sunlight and heat.

The symbolic fall, away from sunlight and heat, downwards, into the cold darkness of the ocean, is seen with great sympathy and approval by Bogeys.

In the Bogey legend, Icterus does not perish in the sea, but plunges through the soft mire of the ocean bed until he emerges in a Bogeyhole. He then returns to Bogeydom, covered in cold, wet Muck and purged of his perverse desires for light, heat and height.

Unfortunately, he had flown too near the sun and his natural green colour had been bleached away. He returned to Bogeydom a ghastly yellow and was known ever after as ICTERUS (Greek, IKTEROS: Jaundice)

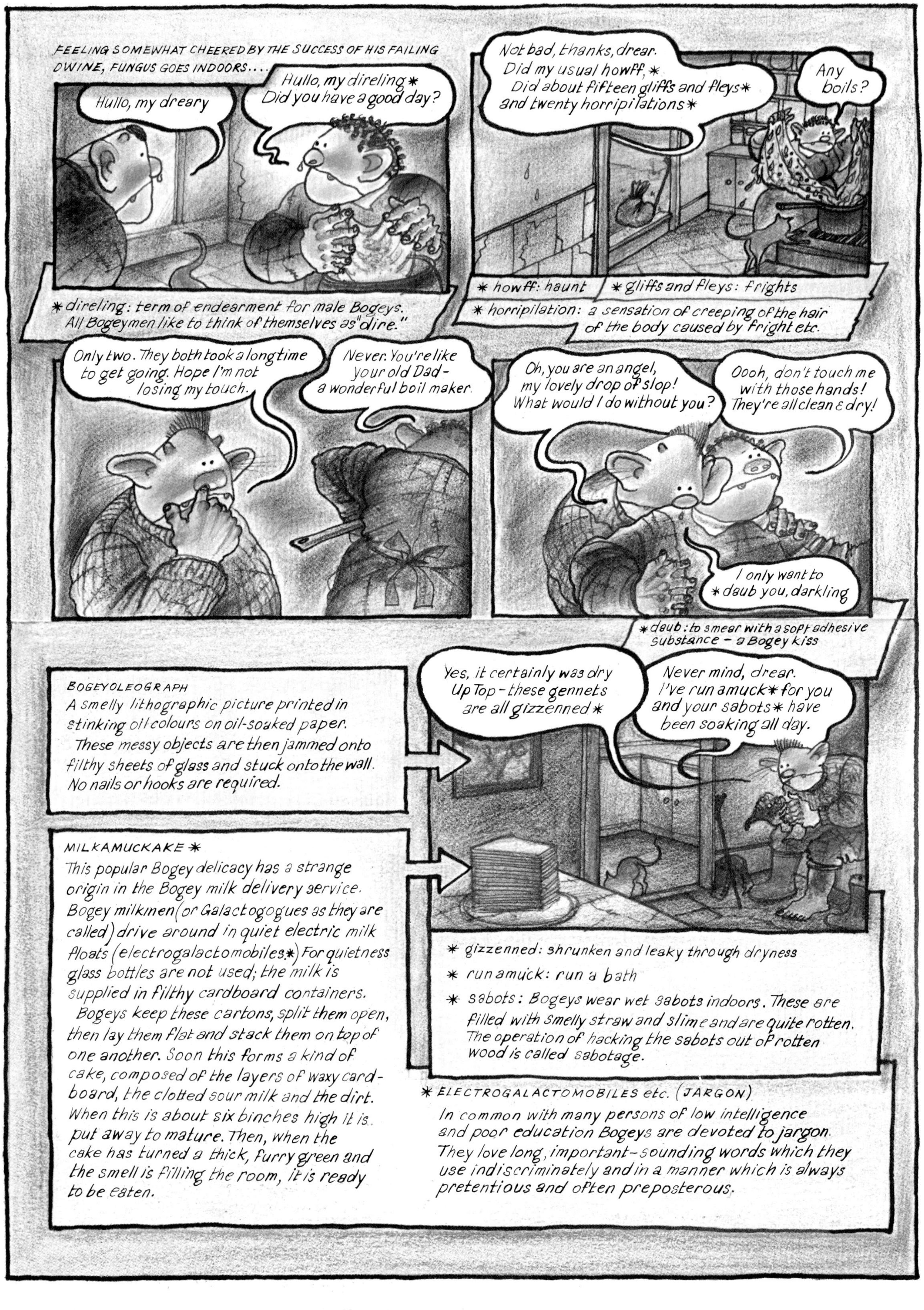
FEELING SOMEWHAT CHEERED BY THE SUCCESS OF HIS FAILING OWINE, FUNGUS GOES INDOORS....
Hullo, my dreary
Hullo, my direling✱ Did you have a good day?
✱ direling: term of endearment for male Bogeys. All Bogeymen like to think of themselves as "dire."
Not bad, thanks, drear. Did my usual howff,✱ Did about fifteen gliffs and fleys✱ and twenty horripilations✱
Any boils?
✱ howff: haunt
✱ gliffs and fleys: frights
✱ horripilation: a sensation of creeping of the hair of the body caused by fright etc.
Only two. They both took a long time to get going. Hope I'm not losing my touch.
Never. You're like your old Dad - a wonderful boil maker.
Oh, you are an angel, my lovely drop of slop! What would I do without you?
Oooh, don't touch me with those hands! They're all clean & dry!
I only want to ✱daub you, darkling
✱ daub: to smear with a soft adhesive substance - a Bogey kiss
BOGEYOLEOGRAPH
A smelly lithographic picture printed in stinking oil colours on oil-soaked paper. These messy objects are then jammed onto filthy sheets of glass and stuck onto the wall. No nails or hooks are required.
Yes, it certainly was dry Up Top - these gennets are all gizzenned✱
Never mind, drear. I've run amuck✱ for you and your sabots✱ have been soaking all day.
MILKAMUCKAKE✱
This popular Bogey delicacy has a strange origin in the Bogey milk delivery service. Bogey milkmen (or Galactogogues as they are called) drive around in quiet electric milk floats (electrogalactomobiles✱) For quietness glass bottles are not used; the milk is supplied in filthy cardboard containers. Bogeys keep these cartons, split them open, then lay them flat and stack them on top of one another. Soon this forms a kind of cake, composed of the layers of waxy cardboard, the clotted sour milk and the dirt. When this is about six binches high it is put away to mature. Then, when the cake has turned a thick, furry green and the smell is filling the room, it is ready to be eaten.
✱ gizzenned: shrunken and leaky through dryness
✱ run amuck: run a bath
✱ sabots: Bogeys wear wet sabots indoors. These are filled with smelly straw and slime and are quite rotten. The operation of hacking the sabots out of rotten wood is called sabotage.
✱ ELECTROGALACTOMOBILES etc. (JARGON)
In common with many persons of low intelligence and poor education Bogeys are devoted to jargon. They love long, important-sounding words which they use indiscriminately and in a manner which is always pretentious and often preposterous.

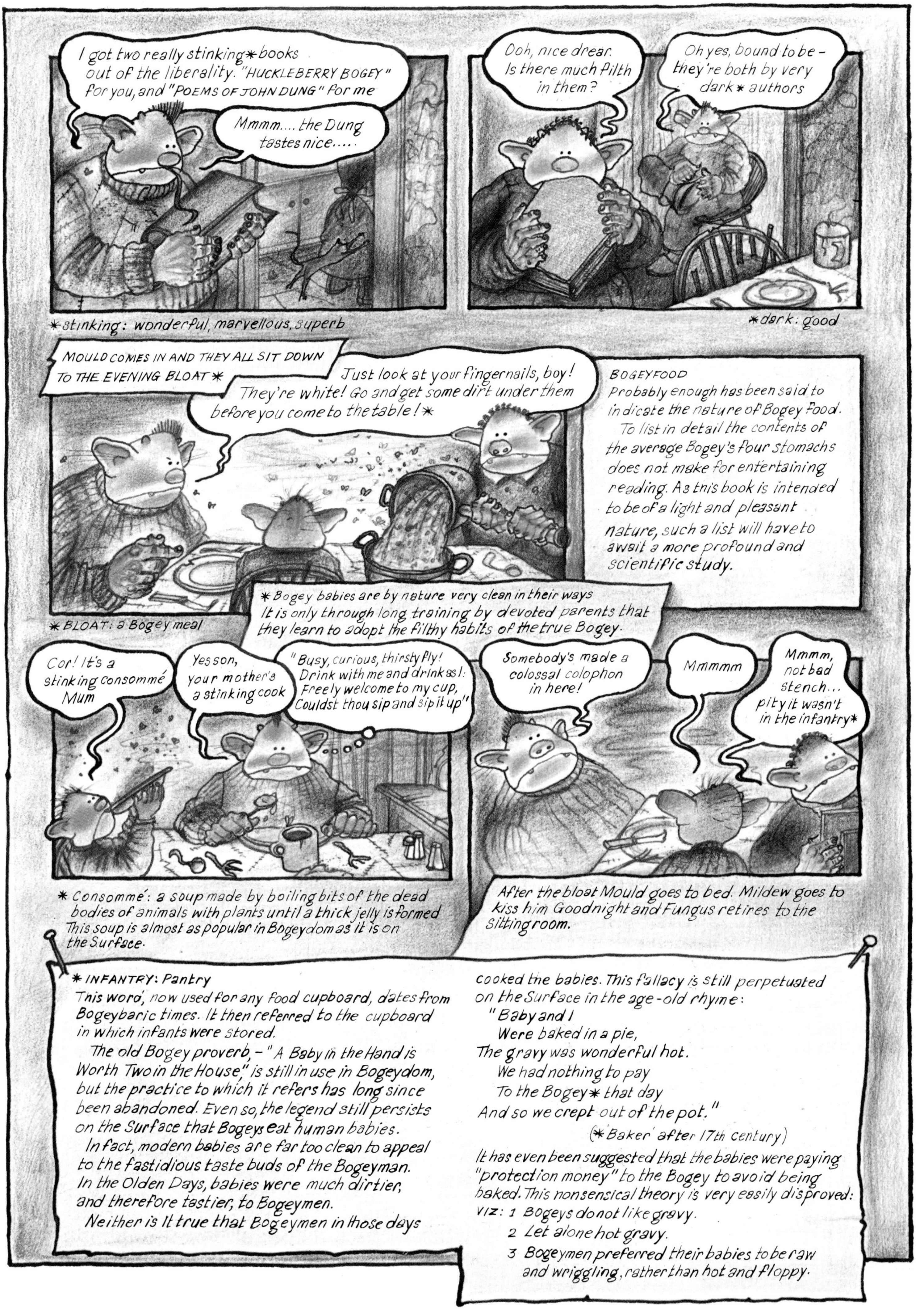
I got two really stinking✱books out of the liberality. "HUCKLEBERRY BOGEY" for you, and "POEMS OF JOHN DUNG" for me
Mmmm.... the Dung tastes nice.....
Ooh, nice drear. Is there much filth in them?
Oh yes, bound to be - they're both by very dark✱ authors
✱stinking: wonderful, marvellous, superb
✱dark: good
MOULD COMES IN AND THEY ALL SIT DOWN TO THE EVENING BLOAT✱
Just look at your fingernails, boy! They're white! Go and get some dirt under them before you come to the table!✱
BOGEYFOOD
Probably enough has been said to indicate the nature of Bogey Food. To list in detail the contents of the average Bogey's four stomachs does not make for entertaining reading. As this book is intended to be of a light and pleasant nature, such a list will have to await a more profound and scientific study.
✱BLOAT: a Bogey meal
✱Bogey babies are by nature very clean in their ways It is only through long training by devoted parents that they learn to adopt the filthy habits of the true Bogey.
Cor! It's a stinking consommé Mum
Yes son, your mother's a stinking cook
"Busy, curious, thirsty fly! Drink with me and drink as I: Freely welcome to my cup, Couldst thou sip and sip it up"
Somebody's made a colossal colophon in here!
Mmmmm
Mmmm, not bad stench... pity it wasn't in the infantry✱
✱Consommé: a soup made by boiling bits of the dead bodies of animals with plants until a thick jelly is formed This soup is almost as popular in Bogeydom as it is on the Surface.
After the bloat Mould goes to bed. Mildew goes to kiss him Goodnight and Fungus retires to the sitting room.
✱INFANTRY: Pantry
This word, now used for any food cupboard, dates from Bogeybaric times. It then referred to the cupboard in which infants were stored.
The old Bogey proverb, - "A Baby in the Hand is Worth Two in the House," is still in use in Bogeydom, but the practice to which it refers has long since been abandoned. Even so, the legend still persists on the Surface that Bogeys eat human babies.
In fact, modern babies are far too clean to appeal to the fastidious taste buds of the Bogeyman. In the Olden Days, babies were much dirtier, and therefore tastier, to Bogeymen.
Neither is it true that Bogeymen in those days cooked the babies. This fallacy is still perpetuated on the Surface in the age-old rhyme:
"Baby and I
Were baked in a pie,
The gravy was wonderful hot.
We had nothing to pay
To the Bogey✱ that day
And so we crept out of the pot."
(✱Baker after 17th century)
It has even been suggested that the babies were paying "protection money" to the Bogey to avoid being baked. This nonsensical theory is very easily disproved:
VIZ: 1 Bogeys do not like gravy.
2 Let alone hot gravy.
3 Bogeymen preferred their babies to be raw and wriggling, rather than hot and floppy.

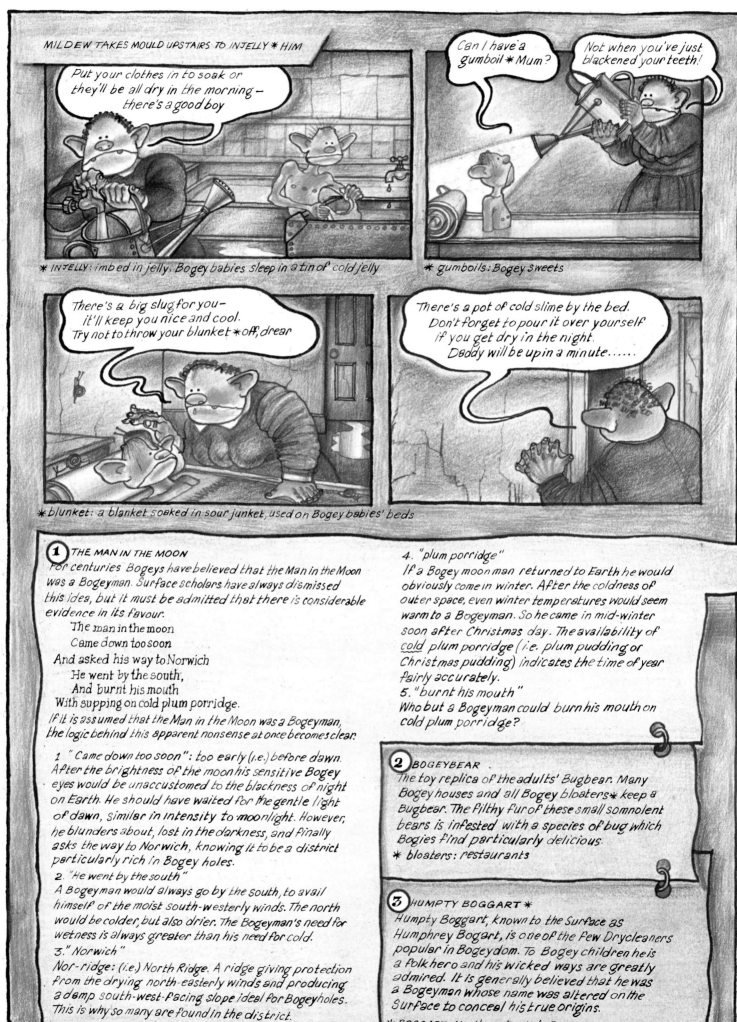

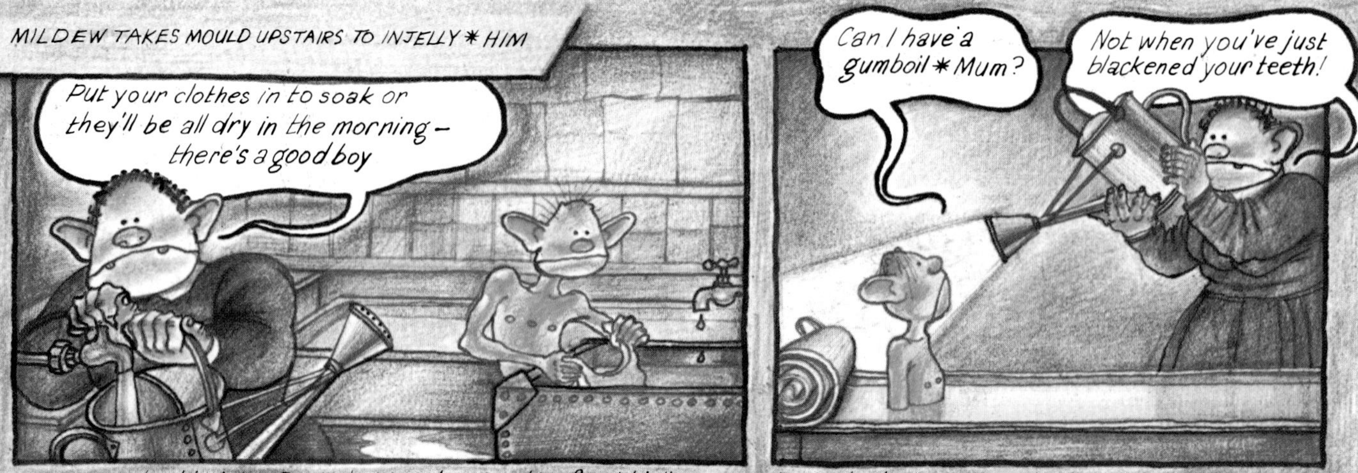
MILDEW TAKES MOULD UPSTAIRS TO INJELLY * HIM
Put your clothes in to soak or they'll be all dry in the morning – there's a good boy
Can I have a gumboil * Mum?
Not when you've just blackened your teeth!
* INJELLY: imbed in jelly. Bogey babies sleep in a tin of cold jelly

* gumboils: Bogey sweets

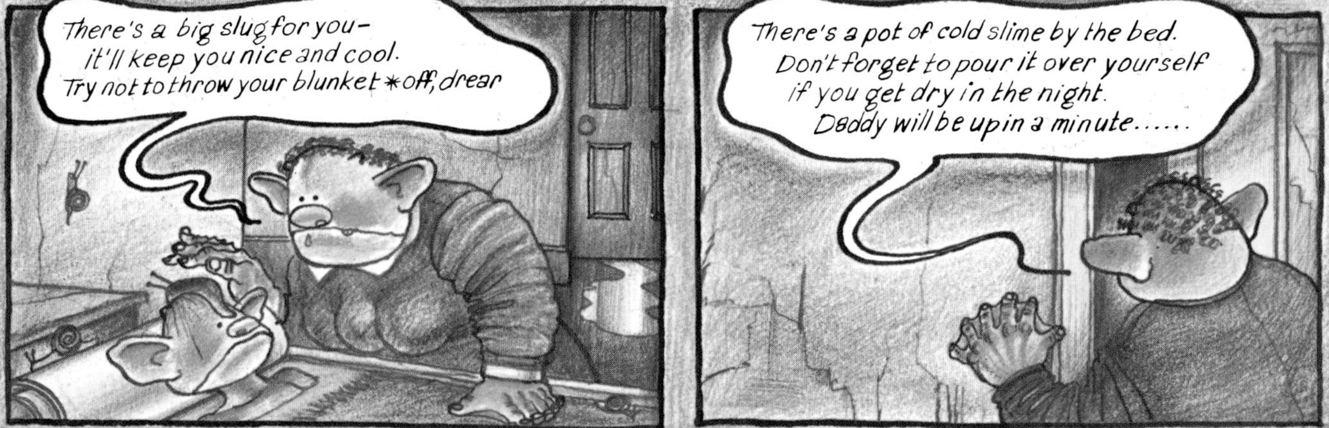
There's a big slug for you – it'll keep you nice and cool. Try not to throw your blunket * off, drear
There's a pot of cold slime by the bed. Don't forget to pour it over yourself if you get dry in the night. Daddy will be up in a minute......
* blunket: a blanket soaked in sour junket, used on Bogey babies' beds

1 THE MAN IN THE MOON

For centuries Bogeys have believed that the Man in the Moon was a Bogeyman. Surface scholars have always dismissed this idea, but it must be admitted that there is considerable evidence in its favour.

> The man in the moon
> Came down too soon
> And asked his way to Norwich
> He went by the south,
> And burnt his mouth
> With supping on cold plum porridge.

If it is assumed that the Man in the Moon was a Bogeyman, the logic behind this apparent nonsense at once becomes clear.

1 "Came down too soon": too early (i.e.) before dawn. After the brightness of the moon his sensitive Bogey eyes would be unaccustomed to the blackness of night on Earth. He should have waited for the gentle light of dawn, similar in intensity to moonlight. However, he blunders about, lost in the darkness, and finally asks the way to Norwich, knowing it to be a district particularly rich in Bogey holes.

2. "He went by the south"
A Bogeyman would always go by the south, to avail himself of the moist south-westerly winds. The north would be colder, but also drier. The Bogeyman's need for wetness is always greater than his need for cold.

3. "Norwich"
Nor-ridge: (i.e.) North Ridge. A ridge giving protection from the drying north-easterly winds and producing a damp south-west-facing slope ideal for Bogeyholes. This is why so many are found in the district.

4. "plum porridge"
If a Bogey moon man returned to Earth he would obviously come in winter. After the coldness of outer space, even winter temperatures would seem warm to a Bogeyman. So he came in mid-winter soon after Christmas day. The availability of cold plum porridge (i.e. plum pudding or Christmas pudding) indicates the time of year fairly accurately.

5. "burnt his mouth"
Who but a Bogeyman could burn his mouth on cold plum porridge?

2 BOGEYBEAR

The toy replica of the adults' Bugbear. Many Bogey houses and all Bogey bloaters * keep a Bugbear. The filthy fur of these small somnolent bears is infested with a species of bug which Bogies find particularly delicious.

* bloaters: restaurants

3 HUMPTY BOGGART *

Humpty Boggart, known to the Surface as Humphrey Bogart, is one of the few Drycleaners popular in Bogeydom. To Bogey children he is a folk hero and his wicked ways are greatly admired. It is generally believed that he was a Bogeyman whose name was altered on the Surface to conceal his true origins.

* BOGGART: Northern English; Bogey, Bogle, Hobgoblin

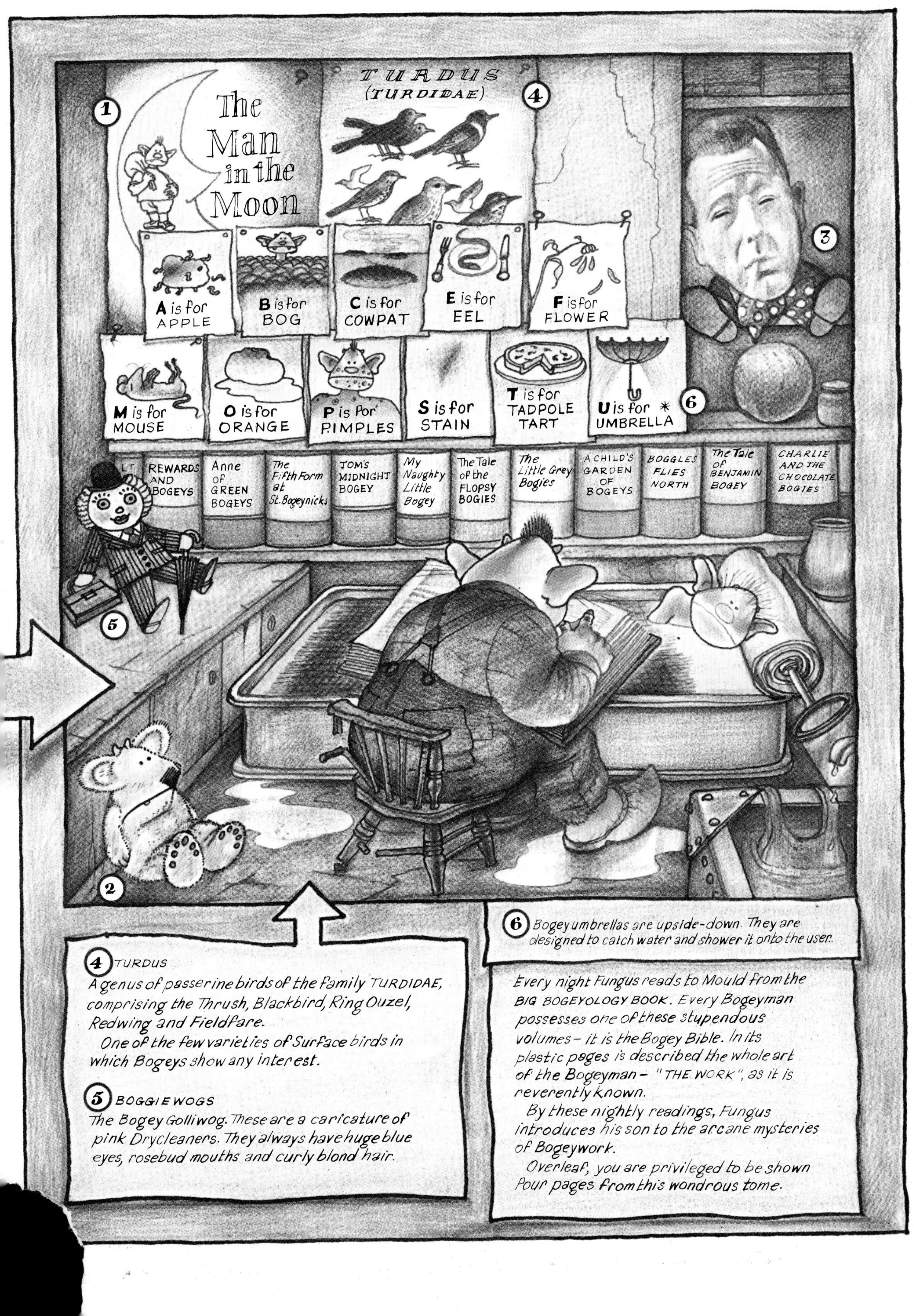
1
The Man in the Moon
TURDUS
(TURDIDAE)
4
3
A is for APPLE
B is for BOG
C is for COWPAT
E is for EEL
F is for FLOWER
M is for MOUSE
O is for ORANGE
P is for PIMPLES
S is for STAIN
T is for TADPOLE TART
U is for UMBRELLA *
6
LT
REWARDS AND BOGEYS
Anne OF GREEN BOGEYS
The Fifth Form at St. Bogeynicks
TOM'S MIDNIGHT BOGEY
My Naughty Little Bogey
The Tale of the FLOPSY BOGIES
The Little Grey Bogies
A CHILD'S GARDEN OF BOGEYS
BOGGLES FLIES NORTH
The Tale of BENJAMIN BOGEY
CHARLIE AND THE CHOCOLATE BOGIES
5
2

6 *Bogey umbrellas are upside-down. They are designed to catch water and shower it onto the user.*

4 TURDUS

A genus of passerine birds of the family TURDIDAE, comprising the Thrush, Blackbird, Ring Ouzel, Redwing and Fieldfare.

One of the few varieties of Surface birds in which Bogeys show any interest.

5 BOGGIEWOGS

The Bogey Golliwog. These are a caricature of pink Drycleaners. They always have huge blue eyes, rosebud mouths and curly blond hair.

Every night Fungus reads to Mould from the BIG BOGEYOLOGY BOOK. Every Bogeyman possesses one of these stupendous volumes – it is the Bogey Bible. In its plastic pages is described the whole art of the Bogeyman – "THE WORK", as it is reverently known.

By these nightly readings, Fungus introduces his son to the arcane mysteries of Bogeywork.

Overleaf, you are privileged to be shown four pages from this wondrous tome.

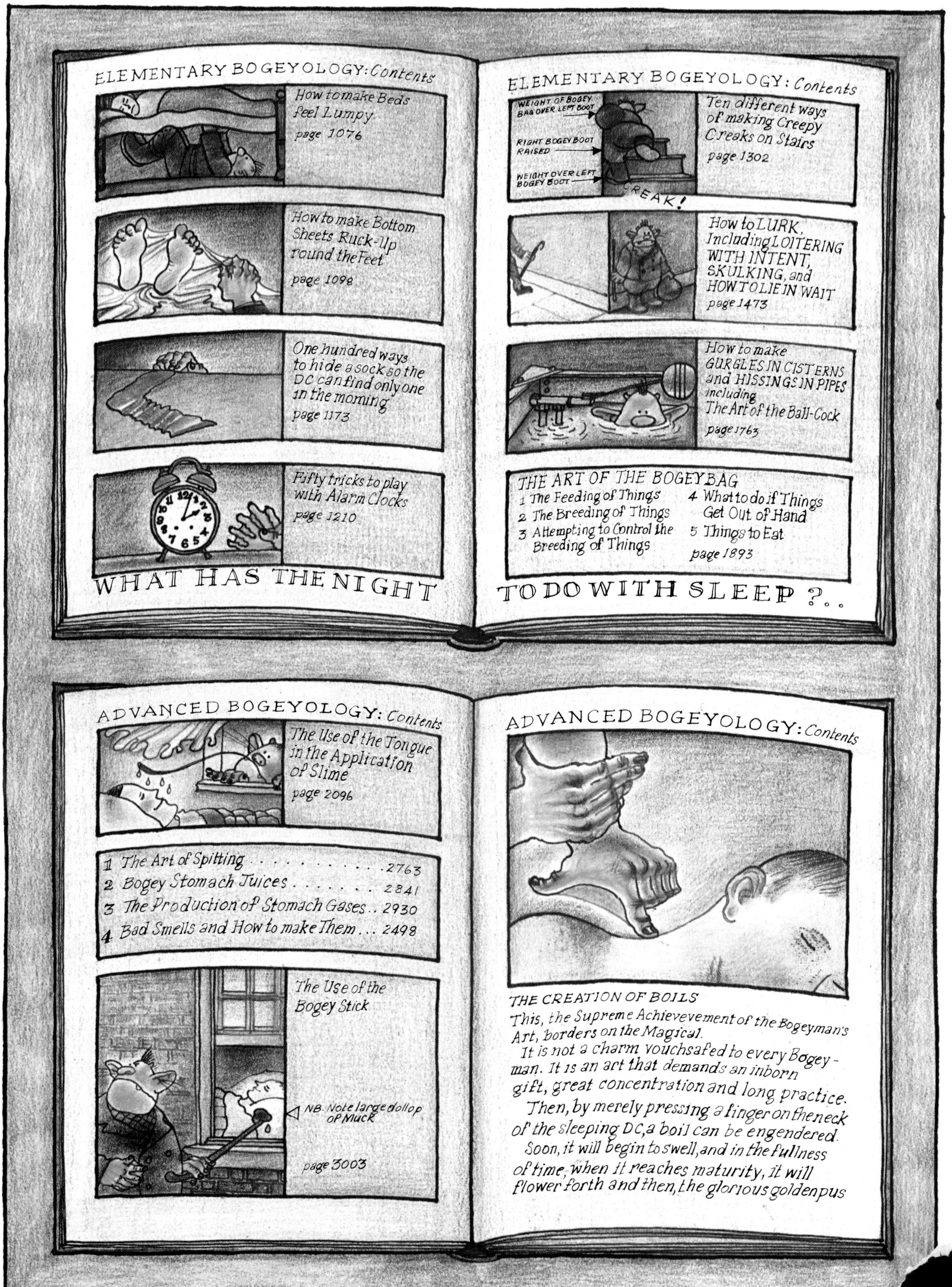
ELEMENTARY BOGEYOLOGY: Contents
How to make Beds feel Lumpy
page 1076
How to make Bottom Sheets Ruck-Up round the Feet
page 1098
One hundred ways to hide a sock so the DC can find only one in the morning
page 1173
Fifty tricks to play with Alarm Clocks
page 1210
WHAT HAS THE NIGHT
ELEMENTARY BOGEYOLOGY: Contents
WEIGHT OF BOGEY BAG OVER LEFT BOOT
RIGHT BOGEY BOOT RAISED
WEIGHT OVER LEFT BOGEY BOOT
CREAK!
Ten different ways of making Creepy Creaks on Stairs
page 1302
How to LURK, Including LOITERING WITH INTENT, SKULKING, and HOW TO LIE IN WAIT
page 1473
How to make GURGLES IN CISTERNS and HISSINGS IN PIPES including The Art of the Ball-Cock
page 1763
THE ART OF THE BOGEY BAG
1 The Feeding of Things
2 The Breeding of Things
3 Attempting to Control the Breeding of Things
4 What to do if Things Get Out of Hand
5 Things to Eat
page 1893
TO DO WITH SLEEP?..
ADVANCED BOGEYOLOGY: Contents
The Use of the Tongue in the Application of Slime
page 2096
1 The Art of Spitting 2763
2 Bogey Stomach Juices 2841
3 The Production of Stomach Gases .. 2930
4 Bad Smells and How to make Them ... 2498
The Use of the Bogey Stick
NB. Note large dollop of Muck
page 3003
ADVANCED BOGEYOLOGY: Contents
THE CREATION OF BOILS
This, the Supreme Achievevement of the Bogeyman's Art, borders on the Magical.
It is not a charm vouchsafed to every Bogeyman. It is an art that demands an inborn gift, great concentration and long practice.
Then, by merely pressing a finger on the neck of the sleeping DC, a boil can be engendered.
Soon, it will begin to swell, and in the fullness of time, when it reaches maturity, it will flower forth and then, the glorious golden pus

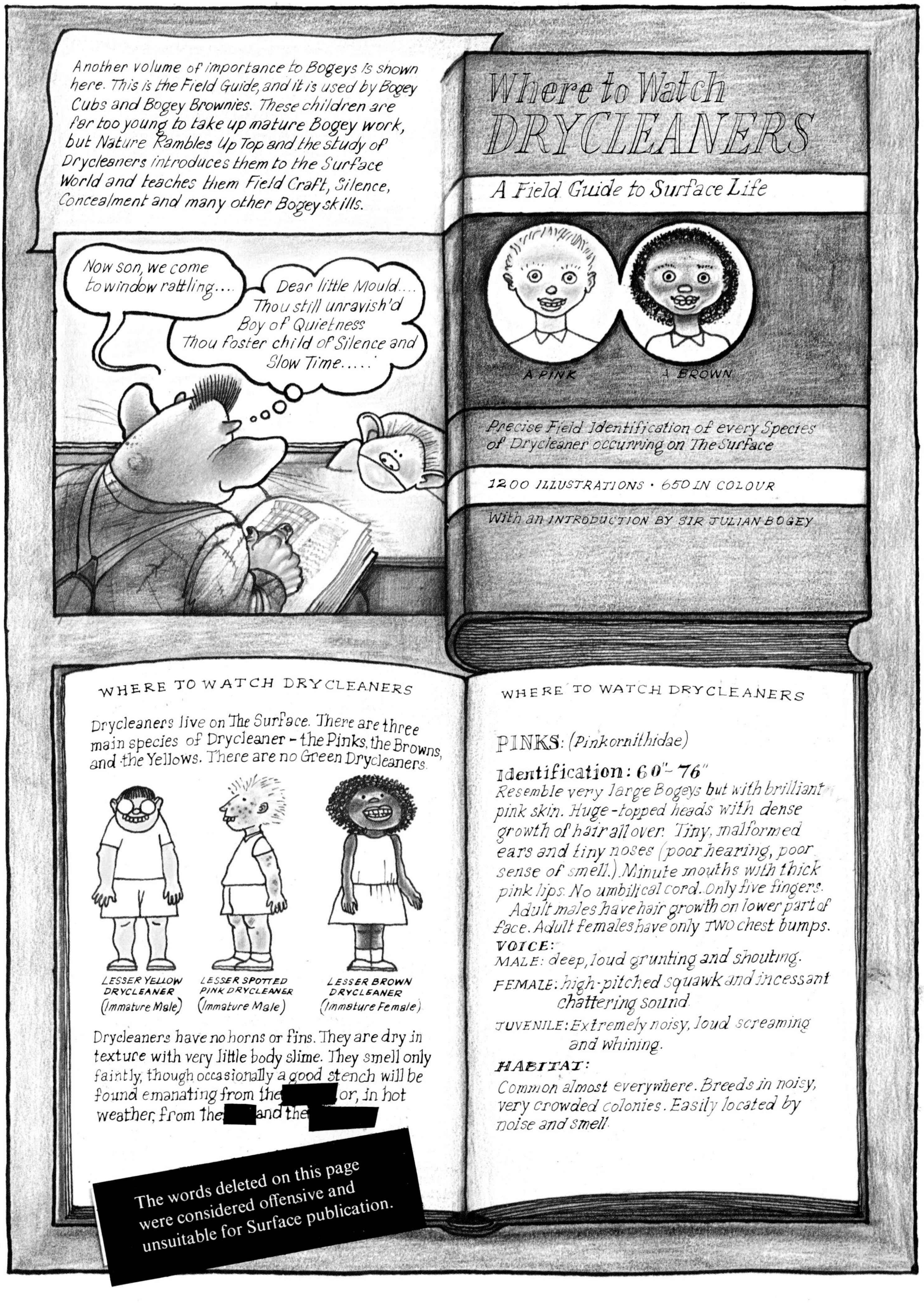
Another volume of importance to Bogeys is shown here. This is the Field Guide, and it is used by Bogey Cubs and Bogey Brownies. These children are far too young to take up mature Bogey work, but Nature Rambles Up Top and the study of Drycleaners introduces them to the Surface World and teaches them Field Craft, Silence, Concealment and many other Bogey skills.
Now son, we come to window rattling....
Dear little Mould.... Thou still unravish'd Boy of Quietness Thou foster child of Silence and Slow Time.....'
Where to Watch DRYCLEANERS
A Field Guide to Surface Life
A PINK
A BROWN
Precise Field Identification of every Species of Drycleaner occurring on The Surface
1200 ILLUSTRATIONS · 650 IN COLOUR
With an INTRODUCTION BY SIR JULIAN BOGEY
WHERE TO WATCH DRYCLEANERS
Drycleaners live on The Surface. There are three main species of Drycleaner – the Pinks, the Browns, and the Yellows. There are no Green Drycleaners.
LESSER YELLOW DRYCLEANER (Immature Male)
LESSER SPOTTED PINK DRYCLEANER (Immature Male)
LESSER BROWN DRYCLEANER (Immature Female)
Drycleaners have no horns or fins. They are dry in texture with very little body slime. They smell only faintly, though occasionally a good stench will be found emanating from the [redacted] or, in hot weather, from the [redacted] and the [redacted]
WHERE TO WATCH DRYCLEANERS
PINKS: (Pinkornithidae)
Identification: 6'0"–7'6"
Resemble very large Bogeys but with brilliant pink skin. Huge-topped heads with dense growth of hair all over. Tiny, malformed ears and tiny noses (poor hearing, poor sense of smell.) Minute mouths with thick pink lips. No umbilical cord. Only five fingers.
Adult males have hair growth on lower part of face. Adult females have only TWO chest bumps.
VOICE:
MALE: deep, loud grunting and shouting.
FEMALE: high-pitched squawk and incessant chattering sound.
JUVENILE: Extremely noisy, loud screaming and whining.
HABITAT:
Common almost everywhere. Breeds in noisy, very crowded colonies. Easily located by noise and smell.
The words deleted on this page were considered offensive and unsuitable for Surface publication.

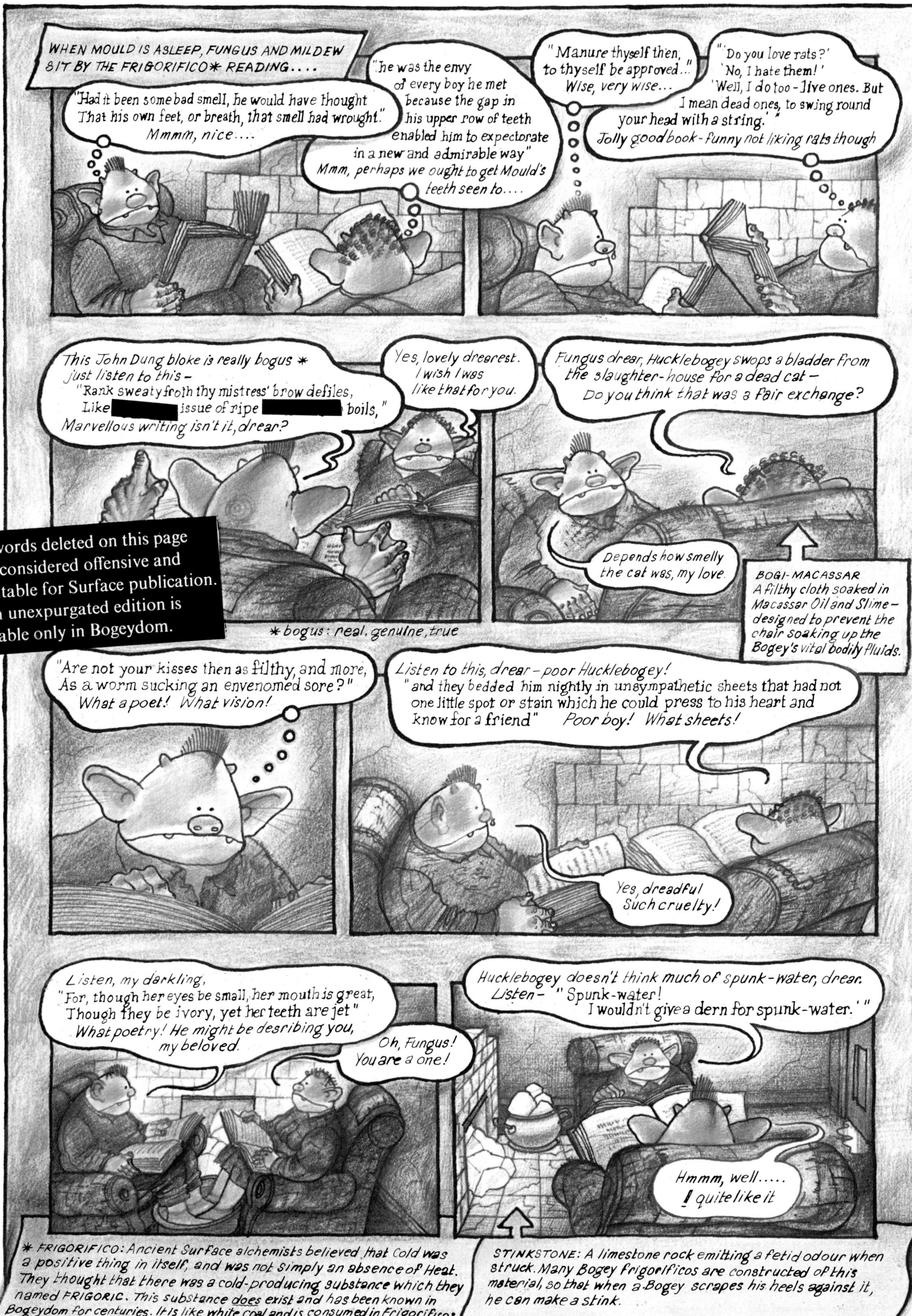
WHEN MOULD IS ASLEEP, FUNGUS AND MILDEW SIT BY THE FRIGORIFICO* READING....
"Had it been some bad smell, he would have thought That his own feet, or breath, that smell had wrought." Mmmm, nice....
"he was the envy of every boy he met because the gap in his upper row of teeth enabled him to expectorate in a new and admirable way" Mmm, perhaps we ought to get Mould's teeth seen to....
"Manure thyself then, to thyself be approved.." Wise, very wise...
"'Do you love rats?' 'No, I hate them!' 'Well, I do too - live ones. But I mean dead ones, to swing round your head with a string.'" Jolly good book - funny not liking rats though
This John Dung bloke is really bogus * just listen to this - "Rank sweaty froth thy mistress' brow defiles, Like [redacted] issue of ripe [redacted] boils," Marvellous writing isn't it, drear?
Yes, lovely drearest. I wish I was like that for you.
Fungus drear, Hucklebogey swops a bladder from the slaughter-house for a dead cat - Do you think that was a fair exchange?
Depends how smelly the cat was, my love.
BOGI-MACASSAR A filthy cloth soaked in Macassar Oil and Slime - designed to prevent the chair soaking up the Bogey's vital bodily fluids.
* bogus: real, genuine, true
"Are not your kisses then as filthy, and more, As a worm sucking an envenomed sore?" What a poet! What vision!
Listen to this, drear - poor Hucklebogey! "and they bedded him nightly in unsympathetic sheets that had not one little spot or stain which he could press to his heart and know for a friend" Poor boy! What sheets!
Yes, dreadful Such cruelty!
Listen, my darkling, "For, though her eyes be small, her mouth is great, Though they be ivory, yet her teeth are jet" What poetry! He might be desribing you, my beloved.
Oh, Fungus! You are a one!
Hucklebogey doesn't think much of spunk-water, drear. Listen - "Spunk-water! I wouldn't give a dern for spunk-water.'"
Hmmm, well..... I quite like it
* FRIGORIFICO: Ancient Surface alchemists believed that Cold was a positive thing in itself, and was not simply an absence of Heat. They thought that there was a cold-producing substance which they named FRIGORIC. This substance does exist and has been known in Bogeydom for centuries. It is like white coal and is consumed in Frigorificos.
STINKSTONE: A limestone rock emitting a fetid odour when struck. Many Bogey frigorificos are constructed of this material, so that when a Bogey scrapes his heels against it, he can make a stink.

The words deleted on this page were considered offensive and unsuitable for Surface publication. An unexpurgated edition is available only in Bogeydom.

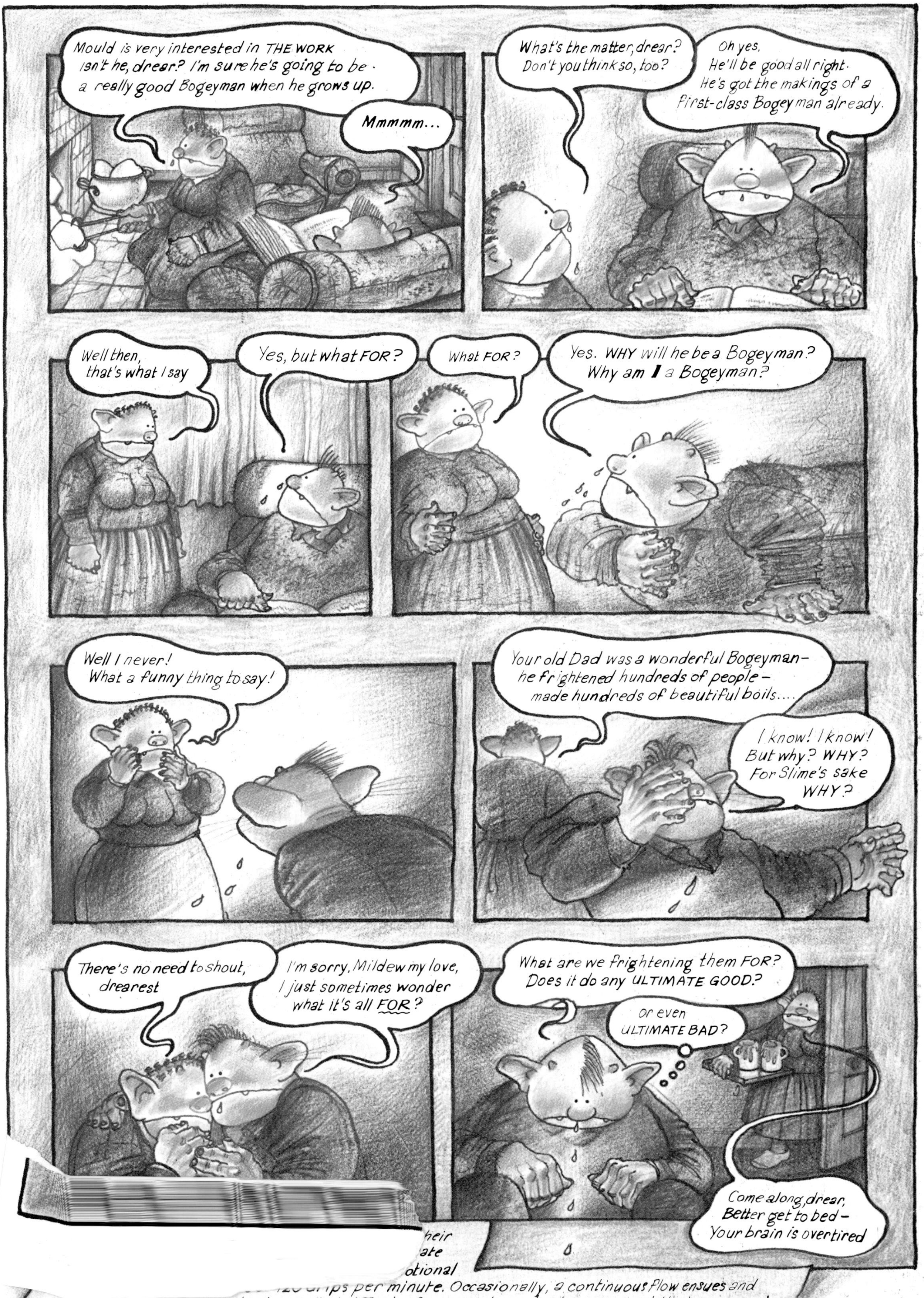

Mould is very interested in THE WORK isn't he, drear? I'm sure he's going to be a really good Bogeyman when he grows up.
Mmmmm...
What's the matter, drear? Don't you think so, too?
Oh yes. He'll be good all right. He's got the makings of a first-class Bogeyman already.
Well then, that's what I say
Yes, but what FOR?
What FOR?
Yes. WHY will he be a Bogeyman? Why am I a Bogeyman?
Well I never! What a funny thing to say!
Your old Dad was a wonderful Bogeyman – he frightened hundreds of people – made hundreds of beautiful boils....
I know! I know! But why? WHY? For Slime's sake WHY?
There's no need to shout, drearest
I'm sorry, Mildew my love, I just sometimes wonder what it's all FOR?
What are we frightening them FOR? Does it do any ULTIMATE GOOD?
Or even ULTIMATE BAD?
Come along, drear, Better get to bed – Your brain is overtired
heir
ate
otional
120 drips per minute. Occasionally, a continuous flow ensues and upwards of 3 pints of mucus has been collected. This is, of course, watery colourless mucus, not thick green snot.

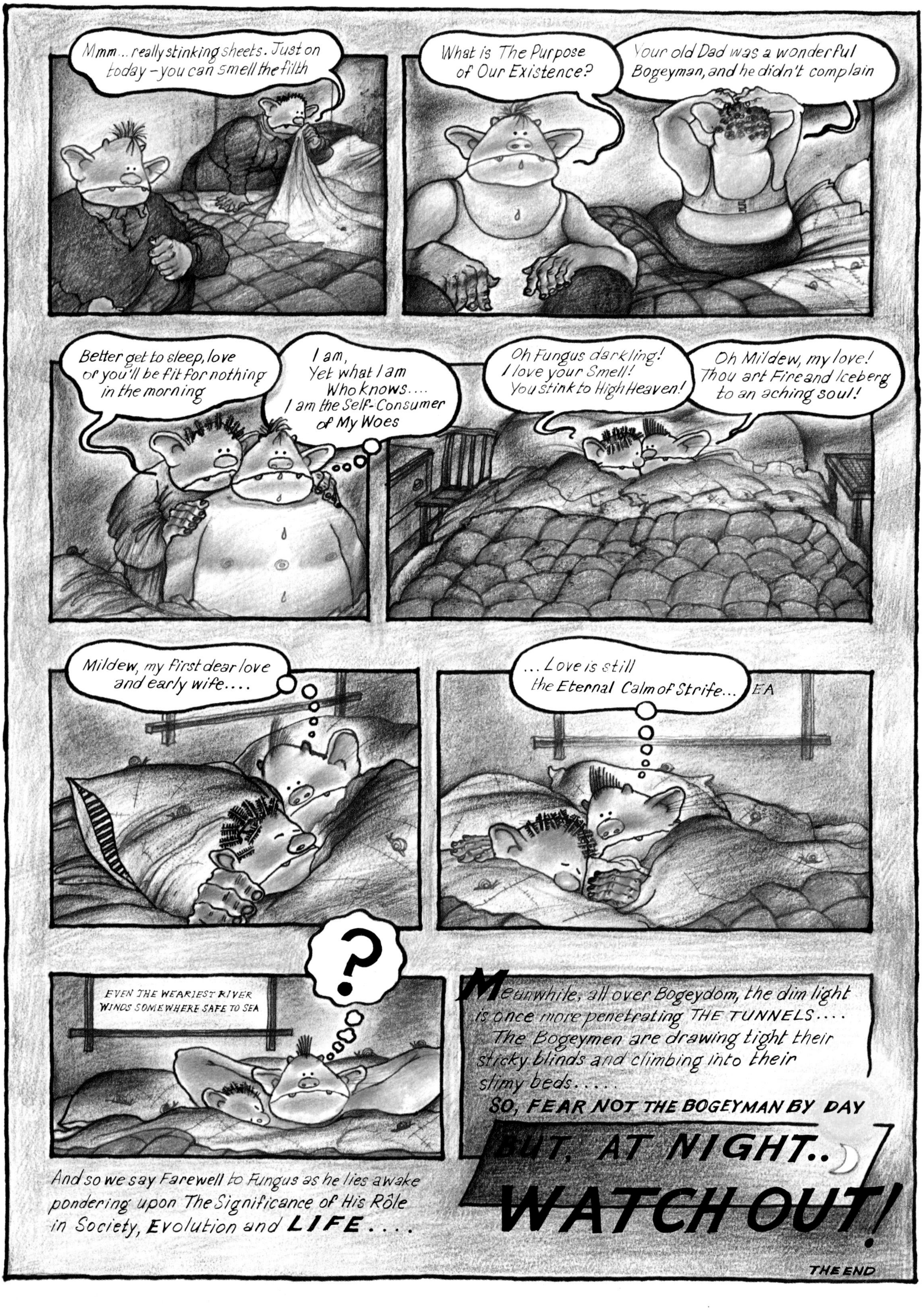

Mmm... really stinking sheets. Just on today - you can smell the filth
What is The Purpose of Our Existence?
Your old Dad was a wonderful Bogeyman, and he didn't complain
Better get to sleep, love or you'll be fit for nothing in the morning
I am, Yet what I am Who knows.... I am the Self-Consumer of My Woes
Oh Fungus darkling! I love your Smell! You stink to High Heaven!
Oh Mildew, my love! Thou art Fire and Iceberg to an aching soul!
Mildew, my First dear love and early wife....
... Love is still the Eternal Calm of Strife...
EA
EVEN THE WEARIEST RIVER WINDS SOMEWHERE SAFE TO SEA
?
And so we say Farewell to Fungus as he lies awake pondering upon The Significance of His Rôle in Society, Evolution and LIFE....
Meanwhile, all over Bogeydom, the dim light is once more penetrating THE TUNNELS.... The Bogeymen are drawing tight their sticky blinds and climbing into their slimy beds.....
SO, FEAR NOT THE BOGEYMAN BY DAY
BUT, AT NIGHT..
WATCH OUT!
THE END

THE BOGEY

The last charge,....he lives
A dirty life. Here I could shelter him
With noble and right-reverend precedents,
And show by sanction of authority
That 'tis a very honourable thing
To thrive by dirty ways. But let me rest
On better ground the unanswerable defence.
The Bogey is a philosopher, who knows
No prejudice. Dirt ?... 'Cleaner, what is dirt?
If matter,....why the delicate dish that tempts
An o'ergorged Epicure to the last morsel
That stuffs him to the throat-gates, is no more.
If matter be not, but as Sages say,
Spirit is all, and all things visible
Are one, the infinitely modified,
Think, 'Cleaner, what that Bogey is, and the mire
Wherein he stands knee-deep!

ROBERT SOUTHEY

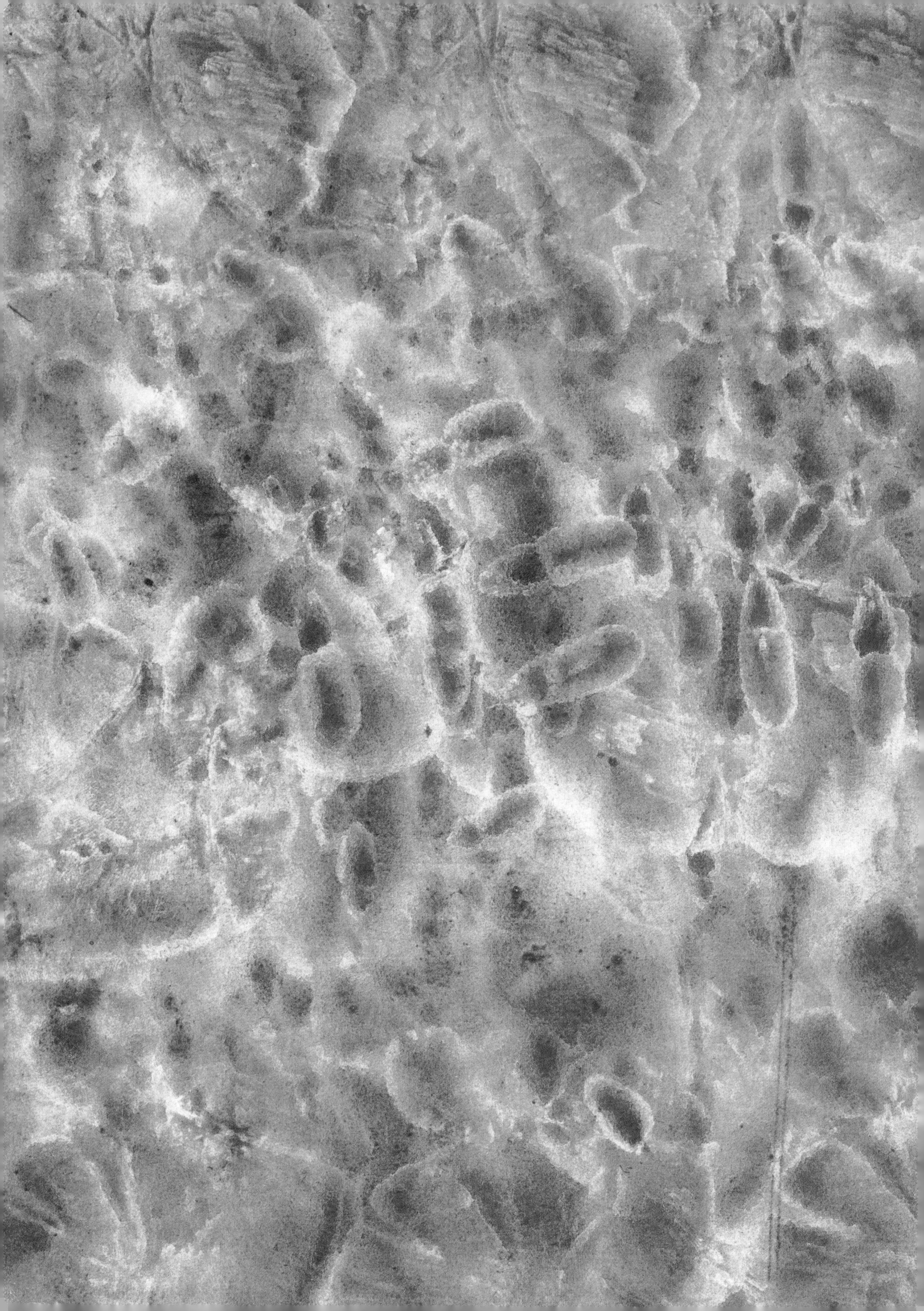

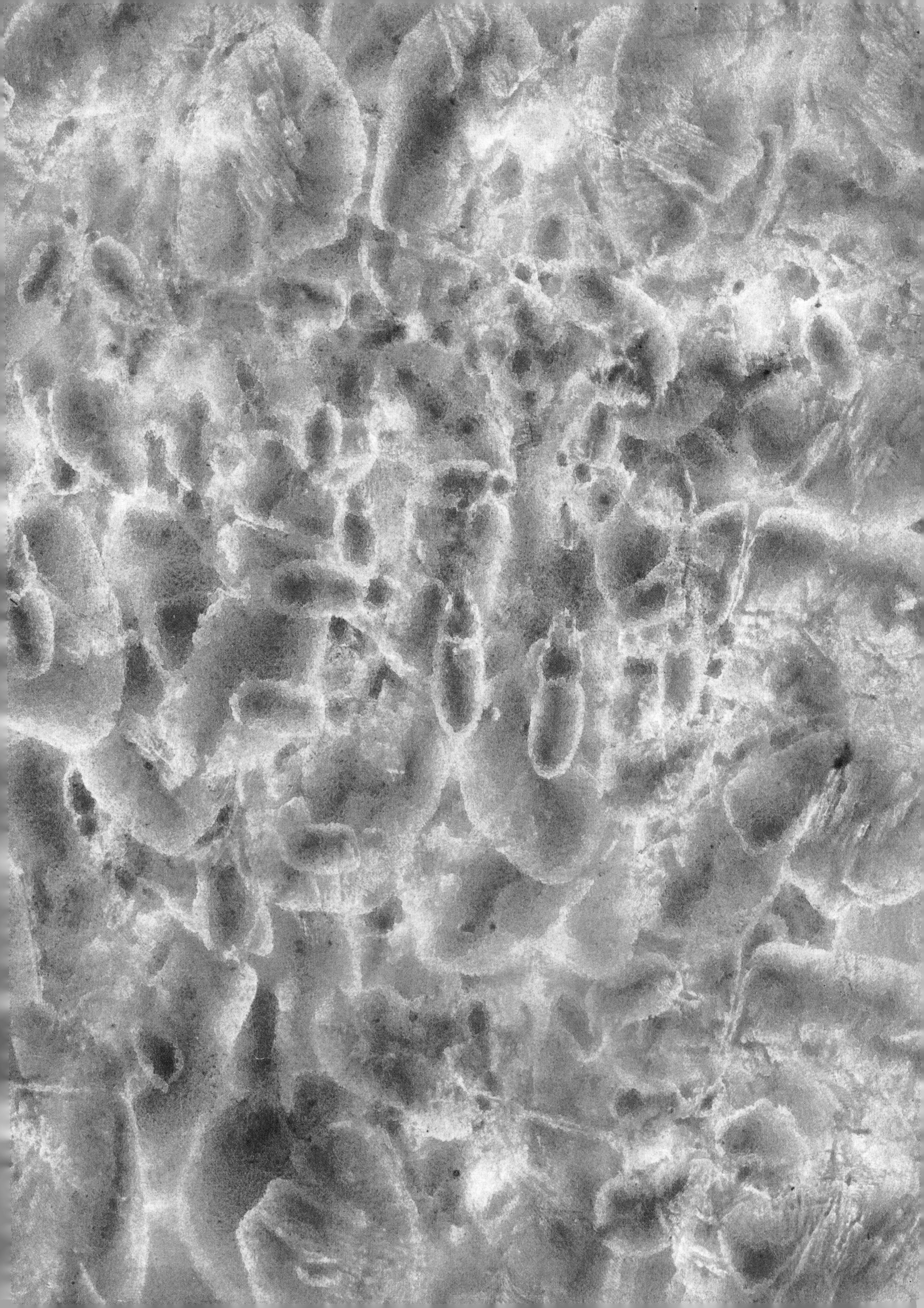

Some other picture books by Raymond Briggs

FATHER CHRISTMAS
FATHER CHRISTMAS GOES ON HOLIDAY
JIM AND THE BEANSTALK
THE SNOWMAN
THE SNOWMAN PICTURE BOOK

Some picture books illustrated by Raymond Briggs

THE ADVENTURES OF BERT   *Allan Ahlberg*
A BIT MORE BERT   *Allan Ahlberg*
THE ELEPHANT AND THE BAD BABY   *Elfrida Vipont*

PENGUIN BOOKS

Published by the Penguin Group
Penguin Books Ltd, 80 Strand, London WC2R 0RL, England
Penguin Group (USA) Inc., 375 Hudson Street, New York, New York 10014, USA
Penguin Group (Canada), 90 Eglinton Avenue East, Suite 700, Toronto, Ontario, Canada M4P 2Y3
(a division of Pearson Penguin Canada Inc.)
Penguin Ireland, 25 St Stephen's Green, Dublin 2, Ireland (a division of Penguin Books Ltd)
Penguin Group (Australia) Ltd, 707 Collins Street, Melbourne, Victoria 3008, Australia
(a division of Pearson Australia Group Pty Ltd)
Penguin Books India Pvt Ltd, 11 Community Centre, Panchsheel Park, New Delhi – 110 017, India
Penguin Group (NZ), 67 Apollo Drive, Rosedale, Auckland 0632, New Zealand
(a division of Pearson New Zealand Ltd)
Penguin Books (South Africa) (Pty) Ltd, Block D, Rosebank Office Park,
181 Jan Smuts Avenue, Parktown North, Gauteng 2193, South Africa

Penguin Books Ltd, Registered Offices: 80 Strand, London WC2R 0RL, England

puffinbooks.com

First published by Hamish Hamilton Ltd 1977
Published in Picture Puffins 1990
Published in Penguin Books 1993
This edition published 2012
005

Made and printed in China

British Library Cataloguing in Publication Data
A CIP catalogue record for this book is available from the British Library

ISBN: 978–0–141–34269–6